ECHOES OF
SILENCE

A FRONTLINES NOVELLA

MARKO KLOOS

AND ROBIN KLOOS

This is a work of fiction. Names, characters, organizations, places, events, and incidents are either products of the author's imagination or are used fictitiously. Otherwise, any resemblance to actual persons, living or dead, is purely coincidental.

Text copyright © 2025 by Marko Kloos and Robin Kloos

All rights reserved.

No part of this book may be reproduced, or stored in a retrieval system, or transmitted in any form or by any means, electronic, mechanical, photocopying, recording, or otherwise, without express written permission of the publisher.

Published by Frostbite Publishing, Enfield

www.markokloos.com

Cover design by Marko Kloos

Cover image © Lukas Jonaitis / Shutterstock

Printed in the United States of America

<Opening File: halley_D/Personal/Journal1>
<Classification Level: Unclassified>
<Date of File Creation: 17Mar2121 1919Z>
<Last Accessed: 15Jun2124 0957Z>

March 17th, 2121
Joint Base Goose Bay

I've never written a journal in my life. As much as I like to write everything down in the classroom or during briefings because it helps me retain information better, I've never seen the need to do the same with my thoughts or feelings, except in messages to you, of course. But the Fleet shrink says I need to find a way to sort myself out out because I'll go off the rails eventually if I don't.

I'll probably go off the rails anyway, but I guess it's worth a try. I need to keep it together. I have a squadron to run, and the last thing I want the Fleet to do is to take this command away from me before I've had a chance to go out there and find you.

This isn't a journal, though. It's just me talking to you. So here goes.

Andrew,

I don't know where I was or what I was doing the moment you disappeared.

I may be able to check the mission records from the surviving task force ships and cross-reference them with my squadron's log, but it would be guesswork at best. The truth is that there <u>was</u> no moment. I didn't feel a disturbance ripple through my universe, no sudden premonition, no feeling of loss or dread. Whatever I was doing at the time, I kept doing it, unaware that you had just left my reality.

I do, however, remember the moment when I heard the news, once the rest of your task force had returned and word had raced back to Earth from the Alcubierre node at light speed. I recall every little detail of it with absolute clarity. It was a little less than a week ago, and I was right here in my office at the Goose Bay joint training center. The sun was out for the first time in a week, but it did nothing to mitigate the arctic cold that seemed to seep through every crack and gap in the old buildings of the base. I remember the dust motes drifting through the sunlight, and the way the light diffused on the layer of frost that had spread across the lower half of the window. I can still smell the electric space heater my squadron orderly had set up for me to supplement the building's ancient heating system. I can hear the ticking of the old-fashioned analog clock on the wall, and the sound of footsteps in the hallway outside. I remember thinking that the knock on my door seemed oddly hesitant.

I was expecting my XO, or one of the division lieutenants. Instead, my space wing's CO walked in. That's when I had the first sense of foreboding. The boss doesn't usually come by my office, he summons his squadron leaders to him. I didn't know why he had come all the way out to the ATS-13 building that morning, but I knew it wasn't because he wanted to share little command wisdoms, so I waited for the shoe to drop. I had an idea that he wasn't bringing pleasant news because he was cagier and more subdued than usual, but I didn't anticipate having my entire world knocked off its hinges.

As much as I recall the details of the world around me that morning, my recollection of the conversation is fuzzy because I was in a daze for the rest of the day. But I have access to all my service audio logs, so I'm going to attach the transcripts to this not-a-journal whenever I can't recall exactly what was said. Some of it may still be classified, but that's all right because this will never leave the system, and nobody else will ever get to read it, except you once you come home.

AUDIO LOG
0921Z, 3 MAR 2121
LOC: OFFICE/CO/ATS5/JB GOOSE BAY
PART: LTC HALLEY, D., COL HARRIS, J.

<START OF CONVERSATION>
COL HARRIS: Good morning. Do you have a minute?
LTC HALLEY: Of course, sir. Come in, please.
<SOUNDS OF FURNITURE SHIFTING>
<PAUSE: 5SEC>
COL HARRIS: Everything going all right this morning?
LTC HALLEY: Affirmative, sir. I've scheduled the new gun birds for some target practice out on the range. Looking forward to getting some stick time in.

COL HARRIS: Yeah, that's the problem with sitting in the big chair. Too much desk work, not enough flying. It only gets worse as you fleet-up.

<PAUSE: 4SEC>

COL HARRIS: Your husband is on Washington, right?

LTC HALLEY: Yes, he is. Major Grayson. He's in charge of the regimental STT. Why do you ask?

<PAUSE: 3SEC>

<SOUNDS OF THROAT-CLEARING>

COL HARRIS: I hate to be the one to have to tell you this. The Washington-Jo'burg battle group just transitioned back into the Solar System a few days ago. Minus Washington.

<PAUSE: 7SEC>

COL HARRIS: I'm sorry. I wanted to be the one to break the news to you. Before the rumor mill reached you.

LTC HALLEY: What...what happened?

COL HARRIS: Nobody knows for sure. There's no official after action report yet. But from what I've heard, Washington was chasing a Lanky seed ship to get into particle gun range. And then they were gone. Washington and the Lanky both.

LTC HALLEY: They were gone. Gone how? What about wreckage? How could they not know? That ship is half a million tons.

COL HARRIS: There was no wreckage. They were on the plot, and then they weren't. Like both ships went to Alcubierre at the same instant. Only they were nowhere near the Alcubierre node in that system.

LTC HALLEY: Which system was that?

<PAUSE: 3SEC>

COL HARRIS: The Fleet still has a lid on the details of that mission. You didn't hear this from me. They went to Capella.

LTC HALLEY: Capella? They went back to Willoughby?

COL HARRIS: Affirmative.

<PAUSE: 5SEC>

COL HARRIS: There's no certainty that they're dead. If they had an Alcubierre malfunction, they may have come out in some other system. That's the biggest, toughest ship we have. They have fuel and provisions to make it home from a long way out. And they can take care of themselves. The task force left recon drones on station in the Capella system to monitor the zone and wait for them.

<PAUSE: 7SEC>

COL HARRIS: If you need to take some time off on emergency leave, I'll sign off on it. However long you need. I'll sort it out with the Fleet.

<PAUSE: 10SEC>

LTC HALLEY: Thank you, sir. But, I think I'm better off where I am right now, sir. Washington is still out there, and I still have a squadron to get in shape for deployment. When they send a rescue mission, Ottawa is going to be the tip of the spear. I need to be a part of that.

COL HARRIS: You're my best squadron commander. When we go, I want you to be there as well. But I want you to consider this a standing offer. If you find that you need some time away from it all, let me know and I'll have them put you on a shuttle home the same day.

LTC HALLEY: Thank you, sir. And thank you for coming out here to tell me.

COL HARRIS: Of course.

<PAUSE: 3SEC>

<SOUNDS OF FURNITURE SHIFTING>

COL HARRIS: Don't lose hope. The Fleet hasn't given up on Washington. We'll find them and we'll bring them home. Whatever it takes.

LTC HALLEY: Yes, sir.

<END OF CONVERSATION>

That's the transcript, word for word. What you don't get from it is how kind he sounded, and how stressed my voice was after he broke the news.

Why did it have to be Willoughby?

And why didn't the Fates see fit to get me back there with you, where it all began?

I sat in silence for a long while after he left. Outside, the sun was making the snow on the distant treetops glitter as they swayed in the arctic breeze. It was much too beautiful a day to get the news that your husband, the part of your life that makes the whole thing worth it, is missing in action and maybe gone forever. It was a day for hiking up the mountains around Liberty Falls in the fresh snow together and drinking hot cider from a thermos at the overlook, not a day for mourning the love of your life.

I decided right then that I would not mourn you. Not because I don't love you, but because I don't believe you are dead.

That conversation was two weeks ago, and since then, there has been nothing new out of the Capella system. *Washington* isn't back yet from wherever you went. I tried to deal with the worry on my own, but eventually I had to give in and see the shrink, if only to get some help sleeping. That's when he suggested this journal. In fact, he told me he would prescribe the pills only if I also started writing, so I'm really obeying an order here. I'll see him once a week going forward, also orders.

Love,
H.

March 18th, 2121
Joint Base Goose Bay

Andrew,

Colonel Harris stopped by again to check on me. He repeated his offer to take me off the roster and send me home on family leave.

I turned it down again.

I can't bear the thought of going back to Liberty Falls by myself right now. I know that I would just spend all my time sitting in our apartment and waiting for news. Home is wherever you are, and you aren't there. I do want to see the Chief and let him know what's happened—but I can't do that until it's no longer classified.

For now, I can do nothing there. Here, I have a purpose. I need to get the squadron and myself ready. *Ottawa* is the only Avenger that's available for deployment right now, so when they order the search and rescue mission, *Ottawa's* it. When that ship leaves for Capella and Willoughby, there's no way it'll go through that Alcubierre chute without me.

Love,
H.

March 19th, 2121
Joint Base Goose Bay

Andrew,

What happened to *Washington*? This question is driving me crazy and waking me at night, despite the pills.

Ships don't just disappear without a trace.

That fucking Masoud. I'll bet he was cooking up something on the side, like we speculated. I told you there was a fishhook in the steak, remember? The mission was served to you as a "deterrence patrol." I just can't see how a trip to Willoughby could constitute deterrence for Lankies after all these years in the system where they have the longest and deepest foothold. That means he had you on yet another cloak-and-dagger mission. Another secret, luxury colony like Arcadia? Surely they couldn't have done that twice. On the other hand, they kept Arcadia completely under wraps, so why not? But why go to Willoughby first? Misdirection?

Even if Masoud is behind *Washington's* disappearance, it makes me feel a little better knowing you are probably on a mission with the tightest OPSEC and subterfuge. That is his MO, so it fits. I am really looking forward to reading the mission logs and after action report from the Willoughby mission when it gets released. That should be any time now. The brass can't keep this under wraps much longer, now that the rest of the task force is back in system and personnel are dispersing. Too many eyes that saw, too many mouths that can talk, regardless of how tightly they try to keep the lid on things.

Love,
H.

March 20th, 2121
Joint Base Goose Bay

Andrew,

I felt a little better today—not all right, but something close to it. We were out on the range for some gunnery practice. You know it's a special kind of therapy for me to pulverize shit up close and personal with the cannons.

We had new ships to test, Dragonflies that had been rebuilt to serve as gunships instead of troop transports. You'd love the changes they made. They stripped the cargo holds and bolted a bunch of automatic cannons to the floor. You know that the regular drop ships don't carry enough ammo to stay on station for the close air mission for long when things get hot. Well, these birds are different. They have one job, to circle above the battlefield and rain fire on Lankies. Each ship has four 25mm tri-barrels and a 120mm anti-armor cannon mounted on the left side of the cargo bay, all connected to automatic loaders with large magazines.

I was happy to see that it worked as designed. We spent half the day above the range, flying continuous left-hand turns at three thousand feet, and laying waste to the target range until our fuel ran low and the gun magazines were finally empty. Watching the other three gunships in our flight going to work filled me with grim satisfaction. Wherever the four streams of tracers from the tri-barrels converged on the ground, it was like God dragging his finger across the surface of the earth. And the big cannon? One shot every five seconds, but whatever those shells hit just disintegrated. I could see the shockwaves from the explosions traveling outward even from a kilometer away.

Up until then, I had never really felt hatred toward the Lankies because it made no more sense to hate them than it did to hate a winter storm. But as I watched our new gunships churn the ground with their guns that day, I kept imagining Lanky bodies getting torn to pieces under those torrents of death and destruction, and I want to make the sight a reality as soon as I can.

If I kill enough of them, will you come back to me? No, but today at the range, I discovered that it's an okay balm for worry in the absence of other options, at least for a little while.

The rumor mill continues to churn about *Washington's* disappearance, and there is really no place on base where I can shut out the conversations except my quarters—but then my own brain just keeps it going. This journal thing does seem to help a little, as much as I hate to admit it.

Love,
H.

March 21st, 2121
Joint Base Goose Bay

Andrew,

I just read the after-action report from *Johannesburg*. Colonel Harris released that and *Washington's* log to me, which includes everything from that mission up to the point your team was rescued from Willoughby by the SAR group, and just before *Washington* disappeared in pursuit of Lima-3. The Colonel didn't offer me leave again. He knows I want to do something about the situation rather than stick my head in the sand. For top brass, he's pretty alright.

My first response to this intel is that I'm impressed with the efficiency of the seed ship kills between *Jo'burg* and *Washington*. Four kills on the first joint mission! That makes me even more eager to get out there. I also know that *Washington* will be able to take care of Lima-3, if that needs doing.

My second response—holy hells, that Lanky-eating creature you spotted would be a useful pet! Let's have the science division bring it back and figure out how to breed them, then drop one on every single Lanky hive on every stolen colony. Let them be the lunch for a change.

Then there's the tragedy of the colonists who died in the Admin building and elsewhere, the ones whose stories haven't been told. I'll bet you and I are somewhere on those memory modules your team recovered, too. Those were early days of the Lanky invasion, and I'm sure many sensors were still up and running, certainly at the station where we first saw them. But the AAR doesn't give any immediate answers about *Washington's* disappearance, just pieces of the puzzle.

So maybe this could have happened: *Washington* hit a wormhole that was undetected by the rest of the battle group. There's still so much we don't know about wormholes, after all. That means, of course, that *Washington* is trying to figure out how to get back. Is there such a thing as a wild wormhole? We can create them with our drives, after all.

This reminds me of some of those old sci-fi vid shows I used to watch when I was a kid. How many times did ships get in trouble with gravitational fields or wormholes that made the rest of the its fleet think the ship was lost? I used to love those shows, and I swallowed the storylines easily enough. Maybe that fiction really isn't so far from reality. *Jo'burg* was recording *Washington* via its sensors right up to the point you disappeared. There was no explosion, no sign of a damaged ship. It was almost impossible to see what was happening with the seed ship because *Washington's* bulk hid it from *Jo'burg's* sensors, and the probes the task force released in system weren't shadowing *Washington*, but dispersed in system more generally.

After *Washington* disappeared from the plot, *Nashville* nosed around her last known location for more than a day using passive sensors at first, but ultimately risking an active sensor sweep. They got nothing, but at least they left several probes in that vicinity and another at the Alcubierre chute. As soon as any NAC or Alliance ship comes back in the system, the Fleet will know about it. If anything, I'm more energized than ever to get out there and recover the new data the probes have gathered since 25 February, when *Washington* disappeared. I am good and ready to find you.

Love,
H.

March 22nd, 2121
Joint Base Goose Bay

Andrew,

My life is so normal, too normal, that I feel deeply lost some days. I'm two different people right now. The one who does all the normal, everyday stuff I've done for years on autopilot, and the one who is wracking her brains going over and over any possible reason you and *Washington* might just have disappeared. Which is a thing that just doesn't happen. I have read the AAR so many times now, I've practically memorized it. But I keep reading, hoping somewhere in my subconscious that the facts will suddenly click into place and give me the answer I need to find you.

Fact: your ship didn't get destroyed in Capella. There was no explosion noted by members of the task force, there was and is no detected debris.

Fact: the task force tracked *Washington* on sensors and visuals as it reported it was chasing Lima-3 for the kill. Naturally, they couldn't detect the seed ship ahead of *Washington* very well and sometimes not at all beyond your sensor information. But they saw *Washington* moving away from Willoughby.

Fact: the kill was not reported or detected, so presumably it wasn't made.

Fact: you disappeared from the task force's sensors in the normal space around Willoughby.

Fact: you were not near the Alcubierre node closest to Willoughby.

Conclusion: You're still alive out there, somewhere, somehow.

I like to think that I would know if you were gone irreparably. I don't know how I couldn't know. But I don't really know how I <u>could</u> know, either, if that makes sense.

Nevertheless, I know you're not gone forever.

How? Magic, I guess.

Love,
H.

March 23rd, 2121
Joint Base Goose Bay

Andrew,

I went through my MilNet box to read our messages through the years. I miss you, and I wanted to feel those things we felt that got us to this point, recall everything we've survived against the odds. All those times we made it when so many others didn't reinforces my certainty that we'll get through this, too.

The first one you ever sent me, after boot camp, was as soon as you arrived at Shughart with the Territorial Army. We sent each other messages every day back then. It was great to have constant and instant access on or so close to this ball of mud you were so anxious to leave. The only time we didn't communicate daily was when you got hurt in Detroit and ended up in the hospital without network access on your PDP and then got yourself reassigned to the Navy.

When you finally got your new PDP and access, you wrote:

GRAYSON.A/INDOC/RTC/Earth/NAVY

Halley,
I'm sorry I haven't written in a while. A LOT has happened down here on Earth and I can't wait to tell you about it. It's a LOT, really. But, I'm in the Navy now, like I always wanted. I'm at Great Lakes for Navy INDOC.
Andrew

And I didn't believe you at first, because of all the reasons I imagined for your silence, none ended with you in the Navy. I had no idea what was happening, and your days-long silence was a little scary. It's eerily like right now, but totally different, too.

Back then, we were new to people <u>actually</u> trying to kill us. Or I was, anyway. You had already seen some shit with other humans. And we didn't know about the Lankies yet—how innocent of a time that was, even with all the things you saw in Detroit.

Now, we shit magnets have learned a thing or two. We have both been through so many near-misses and more perfectly normal times when we couldn't contact each other that I know, deep down, there is something routine going on stopping you from sending me a message right now. Maybe it's a wormhole incident, or damaged relays—like when the Lankies took Mars. Well, not routine, but possible. Oh, I know there's as good or better chance that there's probably something dangerous going on and your adrenaline is through the roof, but I also believe from so many years of experience that you'll find a way out of it.

There's still the Masoud factor, which is such a wild card. It could mean absolutely anything in terms of your whereabouts and mission parameters. Maybe that was actually a known wormhole, a new, secret node well-hidden because it's in Capella System. I mean, if I wanted to really hide a node from everyone else, I can't think of a better place to put it. But it's not like I can just call Masoud and ask him, and I know he wouldn't tell me a damn thing even if I could.

I just wish I was with you. Getting out of mortal danger would be so much more fulfilling than just sitting here, waiting.

Love,
H.

March 24th, 2121
Joint Base Goose Bay

Andrew,

I am still ambling down memory lane reading our mail to each other, which means I've been in a full-spectrum variety of moods since yesterday. I had three meals in the RecFac today and thought about that day on Luna when we sat at a table exactly like it and decided to get married. The mood of that moment was Decidedly Sappy.

I saw the shrink today and shared parts of my journal, just to prove I'm doing my homework. And I have to admit, it's helping. But, I think it's helping only because I know you're still out there doing your mission—whatever that shifty son-of-a-bitch sent you to do. I don't know if this journal would help if I didn't know you are coming back to me eventually.

Love,
H.

March 25th, 2121
Joint Base Goose Bay

Andrew,

I really need to stop reading your messages until the weekend. My moods were changing so much throughout the day that my students must think I'm menopausal, and I'm only 34.

We got disappointing news today. *Wellington* failed her integrated systems tests again. She's that Mark II Avenger the Pacific Alliance funded and built at Daedalus that is supposed to go into service this spring. But there are so many structural and electronic problems with the ship that I really don't know what the fleet is going to do with her. They can't scrap her. That's billions of Pacific Alliance dollars down the drain if they do, but she isn't battleworthy yet, and it seems new problems just keep popping up. How the fuck are we going to push the Lankies out of our corner of the galaxy if we can't even push a warship out of the launch dock in time?

That means *Ottawa* will still be the tip of the spear for deployment, when it comes. I requested access to your suit logs, which I know were uploaded to *Jo'burg* with the rest of *Washington's* data before *Washington* disappeared. It wasn't included in the AAR Colonel Harris gave me, and I want to know what you saw on Willoughby directly. It's data that is completely irrelevant to my job, of course, but I'm hoping the brass makes an exception for the "grieving" wife. I'm still not grieving. You're out there. I know it.

Love,
H.

March 26th, 2121
Joint Base Goose Bay

Andrew,

Remember Gliese 6c, that SRA colony where you and the SI tussled with the Chinese? I can't remember exactly, and I didn't journal back then so I can't look it up, but I think it was about two years after first contact with the Lankies at Willoughby. It was a stalemate, and your carrier took a beating, so you were all a month overdue. That was the first time I was really in the dark about your survival, and I was worried sick for the whole month *Lexington* took to make repairs, dodge the SRA, and get back to Earth.

Then there was Trappist d, a few months after that. I went through the same cycle of worry and anxiety again only to experience that profound sense of relief and joy again when *Hornet* came back with most of the crew and SI detachment alive. As much as I cherish the memory of those profoundly positive emotions, I have zero desire to experience all of the negative ones that come before them. This time, I refuse to grieve. I know you're still out there. And I know you'll be back. I will do everything I possibly can to make that happen.

Love,
H.

March 27th, 2121
Joint Base Goose Bay

Andrew,

We got new orders today—fucking finally. We're to cut our training short by a few days and get ready for rapid deployment. Everything's hush-hush and nobody officially knows where we're going, but I know it's Capella.

I've been busy for the last week. The work kept me from spending all my time reading more old messages and searching for news about Washington, but every time a new Fleet update came across on my PDP these last few days, my heart skipped a beat. I <u>know</u> I'll be one of the first to get any news, yet...

I'm happy that the Fleet isn't wasting any time. But I'm still in charge of my squadron, twenty drop ships and forty-four pilots, and that takes a lot of focus. Many of those new pilots have no real combat experience. All of them have done a tour on Mars, but you know that no Lanky has shown itself on the surface there in a few years. The whole planet is little more than a huge live-fire training ground at this point. Every time I step into the squadron ready room for a briefing, half the faces looking back at me are those of young lieutenants who have never seen a live Lanky or fired their guns at something other than practice targets. I'm happy to see even the cocky ones get quiet and serious when I tell them they are about to go into real combat for the first time. Right now I am using the rest of our training time to make damn sure there isn't a trace of bravado left in that group by the time we ship out on *Ottawa*.

We are on our way to get you soon, and I am ready.

Love,
H.

March 28th, 2121
Joint Base Goose Bay

Andrew,

I'm busy, busy, busy. Exhausted. Almost all bravado erased from my young flyboys and girls! I miss you. See you soon.

Love,
H.

April 2nd, 2121
NACS *Ottawa*, Daedalus Station, Luna

Andrew,

 I skipped a few days journalling. You are always on my mind, but I've been so covered up with preparations for deployment that I'm not dwelling as much on your absence, which is the whole point of this journal. Also, I'm exhausted every evening and sleep is not a problem at all. My worries are more about my pilots. I know from experience that you're alive and and I want to keep my pilots that way as well, all 36 of them.
 Everything is truly in motion now. I'm on *Ottawa*, though still parked at Daedalus, waiting for final supplies and crew. I came up a day early to get settled in, prepare for my team's arrival, and confirm inventory. So I can finally write you a note. I've got 16 new Dragonfly gunships, all in stark white. That color still feels wrong to me, but I am used to it by now. Imagine if we had had these on *Versailles* when we first laid eyes on Lankies on Willoughby—not only could we have saved more crew, but probably more of the colonists, too. But that's wishful thinking. We just had no idea back then.
 If killing Lankies on Willoughby will get you back to me, I will kill them all, no matter how long it takes. But does the Masoud factor include Lankies or is it just another human conflict? I'm itching to get my hands on the data those probes have been accumulating in Capella.

Love,
H.

April 5th, 2121
NACS *Ottawa*, Solar System

Andrew,

We've actually deployed, finally. There were a few last minute snags with personnel, both in our group and the Euro group, like the kind that got you assigned to *Washington*. The Euros shook loose one of their shiny new Avengers, the *Berlin*, plus support ships. Johannesburg and her support group are also coming along, so it's a pretty massive battle group.

As of this moment, *Ottawa* is en route to Alcubierre Node Capella. (I can write that because it's just going into my personal file and not out on MilNet, otherwise the automatic censor would flag this entry in a nanosecond.) I'm thrilled to finally be doing something to help you get home. It's edge-of-my-seat thrilled, Christmas-when-I-was-a-kid thrilled.

It has been a little over month since *Washington* disappeared, but it feels like a half year, at least. The mystery, the worry, the silence from you stretches the passage of time in my world. But now that I'm actually in motion toward you, time feels short again. It helps that *Ottawa* is a hive of activity, hectic and purposeful. Just like the deployment to Arcadia, when we were sent to recover all that stolen military hardware from the fucking traitor government that packed up and ran when things got hot on Earth.

Between us, we have quite the record of survival, don't we? I just got reminded of Greenland this morning from another of your messages. I know you still have nightmares about that ice cave trap the Lankies set—yet another time you cheated death. I am starting to wonder how much more luck we have to spend on survival, Andrew. Your old messages to me are just full of close calls, time after time. Mine to you are probably the same. I had forgotten more than I remembered because cheating death has been so commonplace for us. We've talked about resigning our commissions before, but I want to revisit that idea seriously when you make it home.

Love,
H.

April 7th, 2121
NACS *Ottawa*, Solar System

Andrew,

We're in Alcubierre right now, and I'm taking the time to write because I doubt I'll have many chances after we arrive in-system. Yesterday, we finished the last bit of in-system messages, orders, and data transfers. I received your suit telemetry! As I said, Colonel Harris is pretty okay for top brass, and he's a really good person in general.

So I got to see your team drop onto Willoughby in the Dragonfly. Hearing your voice brought me such pain because I miss you so much, but also such joy—because I miss you so much. I cried. (I know that must shock you, but there it is.)

I have to say it was really interesting to experience a drop from your perspective as a passenger without visuals and any control of the descent. I didn't much like it. What a difference in Willoughby City! But it has been 12 years and clearly the new atmosphere makes all that plant life happy down there. My heart ached for those poor, unsuspecting colonists whose corpses you found. And I'm really glad you didn't go into the school. From the little bit of the colonists' remains you did see, I know that I wouldn't want to go through the data on those memory modules you recovered. As you wrote in your log, the families back on Earth have a right to know what happened. I just don't think they'll be comforted with the knowledge.

You know, the dragonfly going down and you surviving yet another near-miss is both comforting and scary. It's a reminder (if I needed another one) that our jobs are just not high on workplace safety. (Ha, ha.) Again, when I get you back, we're going to have that maybe-it's-time-to-quit talk.

Seeing the new Lanky-eating creature through your visuals was pretty freaky. I'd read about it in the AAR, of course, but seeing it actually moving was amazing. I can certainly understand Elin Vandenberg's excitement. And I'm impressed with her grit. Not too shabby for a science division nerd.

I know I'll watch the whole thing again, but right now, my favorite part of the entire thing is this exchange with her:

Elin: "Like I said, How are you even still alive?"
You: "Because I'd be in deep shit with my wife if I died."

You know me so well. I am looking forward to the conversations we're going to have.

Love,
H.

April 30th, 2121
NACS *Ottawa*, Solar System

Andrew,

I haven't written to you in a while. You know how it is on combat deployment. You barely have time to grab chow and shower in between watch cycles before you fall into your bunk.

We went into Capella three weeks ago. We came with one hell of a battering ram, too. You would have enjoyed seeing that parade. Three Avengers, six cruisers, a dozen frigates and destroyers, and enough supply and repair ships to keep everyone flying and shooting for weeks. I haven't seen a task force of that size since we threw everything and the kitchen sink at Mars seven years ago. It was the first time I have ever looked forward to an Alcubierre transition.

We entered the chute locked and loaded, prepared for a tough battle. Instead of running head-first into a welcoming committee of seed ships, we came out of the chute into an empty and silent Capella system. It felt like we had kicked down the front door of an abandoned house.

I was ready for war. My squadron was standing by on the flight deck as offensive backup in case a seed ship made it past the Orions. We were loaded with tactical nukes on our wings and prepared to launch strike missions against Lanky ships that didn't seem to be there. It turns out that burning for a fight and then having nothing to swing at is almost worse than having to go into battle against overwhelming odds. I was prepared to throw myself at the enemy and follow you into the unknown if it came down to it. Instead, I sat in my cockpit for two hours with nothing to do but listen to the task force radio chatter before the order came to stand down and secure the nukes.

We've spent years sneaking around as quietly as possible in Lanky space. All of that went out of the airlock after we barged into an "empty" Capella. We bathed that system in EM energy from the moment we transitioned out of the Alcubierre chute. After all this time working in radio silence, it felt strange to hear the comms chatter from so many ships and see the echoes from steady radar sweeps on the tactical screen. We were calling out to *Washington* on every frequency. We blasted the space around us with radio waves from dozens of high-powered transmitters, shouting into the void: "we're here, we're here, come home, come home."

Nobody answered. At first. And it wasn't *Washington* that showed up in the end.

The task force flooded the place with more recon drones than I've ever seen deployed at once. I swear I could have made it from the carrier all the way around the planet and back in only an EVA suit just by pushing off from drone to drone. All those eyes and ears turned up three Lanky seed ships in the end, or they came to us. They were on the opposite side of the planet when we emerged. But no *Washington*, no escape pods, no wreckage. The three Avengers targeted one seed ship each and we got three hard kills using the Orions. It wasn't all fun and games, though. *Ottawa* took a penetrator to our aft section because the first one came out from under Willoughby in a blind spot, attacking before any probes detected it. We got lucky because it abandoned us, I guess thinking we weren't threat anymore. It just kept going past us after it fired. *Jo'burg* got it with an Orion shortly after. *Berlin* took out the second one with an Orion and *Ottawa* got the third one one after we recovered our bearings.

It may sound weird, but the lack of any *Washington* debris gave me hope, and it still does. If the Lankies had gotten the better of you at any point, there would have been a quarter million tons of broken warship scattered all over space and given our sensors something to detect. Wherever *Washington* is now, it went there in one piece, and *Nashville's* probes left in system gave us a telling clue. They periodically detected EM spikes similar to, but not quite like Hawking radiation, in completely empty space, roughly where *Washington* disappeared.. Sometimes, in the same vicinity, the probes detected seed ships, both visually and via light displacement, suddenly appearing or disappearing in the rough vicinity where *Washington* was last seen. You know how hard to detect seed ships are; only a few of these "detections" are definite, so the numbers cannot be confirmed or fully trusted, but the "*Washington* corner" of this system, as it is now designated, seems to be a significant point of Lanky interest.

For us, the interesting part is that the definite detections are the ones that disappeared. The seed ships were in system, and then they suddenly weren't. Just like

Alcubierre. Just like *Washington*. So where did *Washington* go?

We are no closer to that answer than before. But the consensus is that *Washington* did go somewhere intact via whatever invisible anomaly is in this part of space. This new data means that Masoud wasn't a factor at all, unless he's colluding with Lankies. And as much of a sneaky fucker as he is, I'm willing to concede the unlikelihood of that scenario. He wants to win the war by all means necessary, but he wants to win it for his own team, of that I have no doubt.

Once we took out the three seed ships and were sure the space around Willoughby was clear, they let us all off the leash. And I mean everyone—the Shrike and drop ship squadrons from all three Avengers, everything that could carry missiles or mount cannons. We descended into Willoughby atmosphere with over two hundred Shrikes and Dragonflies, all loaded to the max with air-to-ground ordnance. We came in above Willoughby City and worked our way outward from there, looking for emergency signals and gunning down every Lanky we came across.

If there's anything good that came out of that expedition, it's that my green pilots finally got to see combat. Whatever happened before you disappeared, you got the Lankies planet-side all stirred up. There were hundreds of them out in the open, more than I've seen bunched together since we rescued the colony on New Svalbard five years ago.

We hunted them down with a vengeance. I emptied my missile racks and the ammo cassettes for the cannons, returned to the carrier to reload, and went back down to continue the harvest. I know my gunner and I racked up over twenty kills, and most of my crews got double-digit kill counts in as well. It felt good, at least for a little while. It made me feel like I was doing something, and it was a hell of a lot more satisfying to tear Lankies to shreds than to be parked on the flight deck. But by our second return trip, the Lankies had mostly figured out that moving on the surface was extremely hazardous to their health at that point, and our target selection thinned out as they crawled back into their burrows. Somehow, they have the ability to communicate almost instantly with each other across an entire moon or planet. I wish we could figure that out so we could interfere with those messages. We visually located and dropped bunker buster nukes on three of their burrows over presumed underground seed ships, just like the ones on

Mars. I personally flew over the spot where you saw the Lanky-eating creature, but it didn't show itself that day. Being there gave me a little comfort, thinking of you and your conversation with Elin Vandenberg. You are still alive because of me. I believe it.

Once I was out of the cockpit and back in pilot country, I took all the excuses I could to be near a command console so I could monitor the fleet comms. I spent the next several hours drifting from station to station, listening to the ship-to-ship chatter and looking at the sensor returns on the tactical plot. Even if nobody replied to our radio calls, I was hoping that you were floating somewhere out there in a life pod with a defective comms unit or hiding out on the surface of Willoughby with Lankies nearby, unable to send a reply without giving your position away. It was a devious kind of torture, to be relegated to watching and listening, but I stayed by the consoles as long as I could, wanting to be the first to spot a blip on the sensor screen or hear your voice on the emergency channel.

If anyone could make anything happen just by wishing or praying hard enough, you would have come back to me right then and there, because I wished hard enough to give myself a nosebleed, and I prayed to all the gods that came to mind even though I don't believe in any of them. I promised them anything in my power if they would reveal themselves as true AND find you. But the system remained silent except for our own voices, with only the hiss of static answering my wishes and prayers.

I resolved to never lose hope. But I know that when I left Capella without you, some essential part of me spliced off and stayed behind right as we entered Alcubierre. That's where I am right now, writing to you while we transition back to our own Solar System.

Whenever things got dark for us in the past, you were always my light. Now I feel like the void is closing in around me, and I am all alone in that darkness. The only thing that keeps me going is my stubborn conviction that your light is still out there somewhere. And the hope the disappearing seed ships gave me, as strange as that sounds. I believe that your light is just too far away for me to see at the moment.

That fact has made me shut down a lot since Willoughby because I have no control over this situation. I don't know what else I can do at the moment to bring you home, except believe. We have always come back to each other, Andrew. I don't think this time will be any different. But the waiting is so damn hard.

Love,

H.

May 7th, 2121

Joint Base Goose Bay

Andrew,

I have been back at Goose Bay for about a week processing and reprocessing the mission to Capella. I've read all three after action reports from the Avengers more than once. Even though I was there, I am looking for different information from other people's perspectives. I've reviewed all the information gleaned from the probes *Cincy* left on station after *Washington* disappeared. And I'm no wiser than I was. I have reached no new conclusions, made no new breakthroughs that will lead me to *Washington*. All evidence points to *Washington* exiting the system at that point where the EM spikes happen when the Lankies seem to exit the system.

So what can I do with that? Not much, in the end. All I can do in my capacity as a squadron CO is train and manage pilots and by extension, their birds. Tracking *Washington* is completely out of my wheelhouse, and that is depressing. I've hit an invisible wall, Andrew. I can see you beyond it in my mind's eye, and can do nothing about it. I've never felt so fully blocked from action, so completely defeated in my life. I've seen the shrink twice since we returned and he prescribed sleeping meds that are a bit stronger because the previous prescription isn't working as well as it did in the beginning. I need you back, Andrew. I need you back. I need you back.

The only reason I have to go on right now is that I don't want you to feel what I'm feeling right now when you do get back. And despite it all, I'm still hopeful *Washington* will find a way back or finish her mission, whichever of those best applies to what you're actually doing. I do think you're on a mission, one whose nature you didn't know before your ship hit Alcubierre to Capella. If you had known about it ahead of time, you would have found a way to tell me, I'm sure of that.

Love,
H.

May 15th, 2121
Joint Base Burlington

Andrew,

I'm back home, or as close to it as I can be. And it's an assignment.

Ottawa is in the dock for an extended maintenance break and repair after Willoughby, and they moved ATS-13 and the rest of the space wing down to Burlington while they fill in the holes, hammer out the dents, and slap on a new coat of paint. Our schedule has us in training, but it's really more of an R&R break in disguise—we're only using simulators. But my pilots just got a whole bunch of experience and part of the training is reviewing all our flight data, near misses, and kills and make plans to improve our actions next time. That part is fun and my pilots are fired up after that mission. It's a big help to my mental state.

I actually think, deep down, that Colonel Harris sent my entire wing down here to force me to go home because I wouldn't take the leave he kept offering. In truth, I think he's right to get me away from the Joint Base. We tried to find you and failed, and now the scientists are analyzing all the data. But there is nothing I can do to help find you right now until they have a new actionable plan. The more I tried to work it out and find an answer myself, the more distressed I became, but now I'm also more hopeful. My last session with the shrink helped me find the positive in the mission and I can see reason for optimism. I mean, we found definite evidence of <u>something</u> where *Washington* disappeared. My distress is because that is out of my field and there is zip I can do about it, as I think I expressed last time. I've been stuck in that feedback loop since we returned, but yes, we did get a few answers in astrophysics. I understand astrophysics only as much as it affects my ability to fly drop ships, but not enough to solve space anomaly questions. So I am waiting, again. You know how much I just love waiting.

It's only twenty minutes to Liberty Falls, as you know. I'm going to see the Chief this weekend. He deserves a lot more than silence from me right now. To be honest with you (and myself), I'm afraid of breaking down when I tell him. He will be completely empathetic. He knows what it's like to be deployed and lose people in the fight. The Spaceborne Rescue guys always appear so distant when they're doing their job, but he knows you and he knows me, and I am certain of his affection for us. He deserves an update in person now that all the general details are unclassified, and I want to bring some flowers to your mom's grave.

    Love,
    H.

May 18th, 2121
Liberty Falls, VT

Andrew,

    I'm at the Chief's place in our little studio. This is my second night back here. I feel completely wrung out and more exhausted than post-mission.
    The Chief and I have spent hours talking about *Washington's* disappearance. I brought him up-to-date on all the non-classified facts so far. As expected, he empathizes completely, and I have bawled my eyes out with him in the way I have needed to do for months but couldn't while at work. I believe Colonel Harris knew that about me, and I'm grateful he forced me down here to be in a safe environment when I face the possibility that I'll never see you again. It's liberating to be able to drop the facade I have to present while I'm on base and working.
    My affection for the Chief has just ballooned over this weekend. He is more of a father to me than my own father, and I have come to understand—both because he told me and because of his actions—that you and I are like the kids he never had. He loves us like family. And the feeling is mutual for me. I told him so and he teared up and those tears spilled over.
    Together, we are both hopeful and despairing about your fate. It's incredibly helpful to me to have him to share my fears and my hopes.
    I have also been helping him in the kitchen and in his restaurant, doing some of the things your mom used to do. I learned how to make scrambled eggs and pancakes, and how to make sausages. The Chief actually grinds the meat, mixes spices, and stuffs the sausage skins himself—I had no idea. No wonder his food is so great. Learning something new has been helpful for me, too. I'm headed back to base at 0630 tomorrow.

Love,
H.

May 25th, 2121
Joint Base Burlington

Andrew,

I'm back at work and find I'm not quite as satisfied to be here as I was before my cathartic visit with Chief Kopka, as hard as it was for me to be sleeping in our old bedroom again. I've spent plenty of nights there by myself when you were deployed and I was on shore duty, but this felt different. There's so much of you in there that I can't look at anything without thinking of you. That's always been a comfort, but this time it was bittersweet. I spent several hours at oh-dark-thirty holding your mom's rosary beads, counting them over and over. There are 59 beads and a cross. I can spell your name 5 times in one circuit of the necklace. I don't know how many times I prayed your name, Andrew, but it's a lot. You know I've never been religious, and I don't know if that use is a desecration of a rosary, but I'm pretty sure that if there's a God, he or she won't mind that it gives me comfort.

    That visit told me I'm not holding on to my conviction of your eventual return as much as I want to. I'm sure it's a hangover from the disappointing Willoughby mission. But it's there, nonetheless. As great as the visit with the Chief was, I think it changed me in just two days because I actually faced a potential reality I didn't was to admit was there—life without you. Now, any time negative feelings or thoughts pop up, I just want to see the Chief. I'm not grieving—I'm scared for the unknowns about you, and that realization hit me hard. I am not easily scared because I usually have some control over any given situation I find myself in, and I don't like this feeling one bit.

    Before you disappeared, I was a very good officer. I knew my stuff, I was conscientious and fair, I worked hard, and I was one of the best drop ship pilots in the entire Fleet. (I know you'd make a quip about my modesty right about now, but we both know I'm just stating a fact here.) I was on the fast track to colonel, a space wing XO slot in another three years and maybe commanding officer of my own wing in five.

    But things have changed. I have changed. I'm working the same long hours as before, but I don't think I'm a very good officer anymore. I have less patience these days, and I get irritated very quickly. I come down on my subordinates harder for mistakes. There are plenty of mornings where I have a hard time mustering the willpower to get out of my bunk. I don't even enjoy flying the way I used to, if you can believe that. You know I would get behind the stick whenever I could, even as the XO and then CO. Now I fly only when I'm scheduled for logging some hours to keep my flight status current. I never thought I'd lose that piece of myself, but I can feel it starting to drift away from me.

I've lost weight I couldn't really spare to lose. I eat less even though the base chow at Burlington is good. Whenever I do go to the chow hall, I go at odd hours so I'm mostly alone and I don't have to interact with anyone. Without you, the days have begun to feel the same, and I don't look forward to any of them anymore.

Not too long ago, I would have done anything to get the job I have now, to move up through the ranks and take on even bigger responsibilities, maybe become a general officer one day. Now I think about the eight years we both still need serve until our full retirement package kicks in, and I feel only exhaustion. Maybe I need an extended maintenance break as well. Not that I think they'll be able to get me back to shiny and new condition. I'm certain that the dents I got in the last few months are beyond their ability to fix. There's only one way to straighten those out, and that's for me to see your face again in person. I see you almost every night in your last message to me.

Love,
H.

June 10th, 2121
Joint Base Burlington

Andrew,

Today is a good day.

Colonel Harris and I had a meeting and he updated me on the research into the data we recovered in Willoughby. Our astrophysicists think that there is near conclusive evidence of a wormhole in that area, which means *Washington* is very likely still intact and trying to get back. But where does that wormhole go? The possibilities are staggering. It's such a big universe that even that little piece of galaxy we've managed to explore seems almost infinite.

The next step is obviously to figure out a way to get inside and see where it leads. Astrophysics is designing experiments to test their theories, and *Ottawa* will be the lead Avenger for that mission again. So, there's a plan of action again, finally. Nothing makes me feel better than having things to do, and this plan gives me hope again. More details as I get them. I'm excited to be preparing for a mission, when it happens. And that makes me feel and act like I have a purpose again.

Love,
H.

June 14th, 2121
Liberty Falls, VT

Andrew,

I'm at the Chief's again, but this time, there was a whole lot of hope, fewer tears. Maybe I got all the tears and fears off my chest last time I was here. I told him about the possible wormhole and obliquely broke regs by commenting on the inevitability of a mission to investigate it. And we talked hopefully and speculated about the places you could be exploring right now. I helped him out again—this time I actually took some orders and served some tables. I washed a lot of dishes and chopped a lot of onions. It was a fun and uplifting visit. All my tears were from the onions this time.

Love,
H.

June 27th, 2121
Joint Base Burlington

Andrew,

ATS-13 just got orders to return to Goose Bay on Monday. *Ottawa* is combat-ready again and that astrophysics mission is in the works, although I have zero details yet. It makes me hopeful again, though.

I'll get any available details back in Goose Bay, so I'm looking forward to getting back. And I do keep reminding myself that we have both survived crazy odds in our years in the Corps, that's there's still hope, and that you will keep living for me, like you told Elin. Don't make me kick your ass for being dead, you hear?

Love,
H.

July 1st, 2121
Joint Base Goose Bay

Andrew,

I'm back in my office in Goose Bay, and I feel refreshed. The squadron had a long break and light training at Joint Base Burlington, but the time I spent with Chief Kopka has been the most restorative. I stayed at his place again last weekend and enjoyed helping him out in the restaurant, but especially just his companionship in general. He and his girlfriend broke up, and he seemed to need me to talk, too. I was happy to support him in any way. And I'm sorry for his loss, but it felt great to be needed.

I met with Colonel Harris in person this morning and communicated the positive effect my sort-of-down time had on me. He smiled knowingly. I hope I am half as good a CO as he is.

Now the exciting stuff: astrophysics has designed a wormhole probe with a mini Alcubierre drive to attempt wormhole entry, to figure out where the wormhole goes. This time, the task force will include two Avenger battle groups, *Ottawa* and *Yamato*. It will be *Yamato's* first extra-solar trip, so it's sort of a live-fire exercise for that ship. *Wellington* has failed to pass safety tests again, so she's still not launching.

The Pacific Alliance must be livid. That puts *Wellington* several months behind schedule. Naturally, she can't be scrapped because she's a brand new hull, so she's having a bunch of her neural network hardware stripped and replaced and two replacement engines installed. I've never seen a new ship present with so many problems right out of the shipyard, but her particle cannons both failed their tests and caused cascade network and electrical failures, burning circuits and other critical elements. It's certainly better that that happens in testing than in the field, but that ship was supposed to launch months ago. She's costing about twice her initial investment by now.

Cincinnati is assigned to *Ottawa's* group and Astrophysics will be doing their work from her. *Nashville* is also along for scout work while *Cincy* does her work and *Ottawa* is just the linebacker. The minesweeper is *Thresher*, one of the Hammerhead cruisers.

Right now, the plans don't call for any trips to the planet, but ATS-13 is going along for the just-in-case scenarios. I'm excited to get into space again with at least the potential for action, but I'm really interested to see what Astrophysics R&D has up its sleeve. We leave in two weeks.

    Love,
    H.

July 7th, 2121
Joint Base Goose Bay

Andrew,

We leave for Capella again next week. I've just been doing the usual with my pilots, ad nauseam. As I wrote before, I've lost something of myself since your disappearance. None of this is as rewarding as it used to be. I am more excited about what Astrophysics is doing than what I'm doing. Part of that is the fact that we don't really have a mission on the trip; the other part is that all my pilots have real experience in Lankyland now, so I'm not as worried about them as I was the last time we went to Capella. My biggest job is to dial back their cockiness now that they do have some experience. And I'm sick of that. Maybe I'm just too old to tolerate the bullshit anymore. Or maybe it's just that I'm so tired of trying to stop the hot young flyboys and girls from killing themselves. I wonder if I was that reckless when I was their age? And I'm not that old. I don't know what it is, but I'm tired. I feel old some days.

I've been studying astrophysics in my free time so I can understand what the Astrophysics team is doing and it is fascinating. With Alcubierre drives, we physically create wormholes by folding spacetime in front of us, like pulling a flat linen tablecloth toward yourself with an open hand on the table, creating several ridges. The greater the distance, the more ridges, right? Then the drive literally makes a hole through those ridges, like pushing a knitting needle through them. How we get our hands as far out as our farthest colony to pull the cloth toward us is the part I don't quite get. Somehow, though, the drive is able to fix on a point in space by triangulating on two or more pulsar signatures. The first ship that did this back in the very beginning was very daring and death was a high probability, but it provided the anchor for the chute, so it worked. Now, they've figured a way to send unmanned probes to anchor the end point in spacetime to create the end of the wormhole. They lose a lot of probes because what happens to be at the precise endpoint is completely unknown. They could be trying to anchor on a planet, or a nebula, or a black hole, or any number of other dangerous things that destroy the probe. So almost all initial Alcubierre anchor attempts fail. All the Alcubierre nodes we do have to all of our systems were so much dumb luck, I think.

While learning all this is really fascinating, it keeps you on my mind, naturally. Right now, the best guess is that *Washington* accidentally went through a wormhole that appears to be known to the seed ships in Capella, but that we can't actually see or use with our drives—as far as we know, anyway. Did your Alcubierre drive spontaneously create a chute or enter an existing chute we can't see? I don't know, and I can't speculate with any real confidence because I just don't know enough about this stuff, but Astrophysics wants to know and I'm exciting that they are trying to find the answers.

It gives me a lot of hope again. If we know the place to start and somehow figure out the endpoint to within a quarter lightyear or so, maybe there's a good chance we can made a chute to you and get you back. That thought keeps me afloat right now.

Love,
H.

July 15th, 2121
NACS *Ottawa*, Solar System

Andrew,

We are en route to the Capella chute. A huge part of me feels just as hopeful as the last time I made this trip that *Washington* will somehow be there. But if you aren't, at least Astrophysics will be finding new, stronger clues to where you went, clues that may lead us to you. The Capella system is where we really became us, where we decided that we were the ones for each other, where my complete life began. I don't want that to be where it ends. Please come back to me, Andrew.

Love,
H.

July 16th, 2121
NACS *Ottawa*, Capella System

Andrew,

Washington isn't here. But the probes and Wonder Balls we left behind inundated us with data streams when we entered the system. I don't see how that noise won't attract seed ships if they're here.

Love,
H.

July 20th, 2121
NACS *Ottawa*, Capella System

Andrew,

We are on station in Capella, just watching the neighborhood while the Astrophysics team does their thing on *Cincinnati*. And boy, are these people daring for a bunch of civilians with military rank facades. Not only are they launching a probe from the spot that emits an EM spike when the occasional Lanky seed ship disappears (that's not daring, exactly), but they actually want to tag a seed ship, like it's a migrating shark. They developed a type of harpoon that has a recording module in it. The hope is that the seed ship they tag will go through the worm hole and then return so the massive array of probes in system can capture the data and see where they went. They're using a modified silver bullet, greatly sized up for the ship rather than a Lanky on the ground, and not with an explosive charge to destroy the ship, but with a small charge to push a tracking device into the hull. We know their hulls are like whale blubber for lack of a better analogy, so we know we can imbed something in it and hope no one notices on the ship. The risk is that the seed ship will notice, turn on *Cincy* and start looking for the rest of us. I am a little in awe of the scientists' audacity. But the end result is that we can't kill any seed ships in system. There are three again right now. We are keeping tight EMCON, hiding behind one of Willoughby's moons, while *Cincy* lets the scientists do their thing. They have a specialized cannon probe to launch the silver bullet/harpoon.

This is both the most tense and boring sitrep ever. The only exciting part is when *Ottawa, Yamato* and *Cincy* need to communicate. Because the EMCON is so tight (we don't want to distract seed ships from using the worm hole or draw their attention to the ships), we are using courier Blackflies back and forth at least twice daily shuttling personnel and or recorded messages between the skippers. I'm letting all the pilots take turns doing that.

We are going to be in system a while, I think, because we have to wait for a seed ship to approach the magic point in space before the probe launches the silver bullet. And we can't kill any of them because we want them to go on their happy ways. But we're gathering super interesting intelligence of the kind we have never gotten before. We've actually watched seed ships deploy those pods that are full of ground-based Lankies like the ones that landed on Earth and then go into orbit around Willoughby. They are still very stealthy, but this system is literally covered in probes, the new Wonder Balls, gathering passive data. The seed ships frequently knock into and destroy them, probably by sheer accident, but not before the probes identify them either visually or via light displacement or we identify them when a probe disappears from the network.

This is the most data the scientists have gathered so far and I can hear the excitement in their voices when I'm in the CIC on *Cincy*. It is pretty exciting, I have to admit, and it is a nice distraction from my disappointment at *Washington's* continued absence. These science people are brilliant.

I also have to admit a huge part of me is hoping *Washington* pops back in the system while we're waiting. That may be foolish, but that's what hope does to a brain. Either way, waiting here is better than waiting on Earth.

Love,
H.

July 30th, 2121
NACS *Ottawa*, Capella System

Andrew,

The scientists managed to tag seed ship with a probe! It has taken several days, but they did it!

As far as anyone can tell, no one aboard the seed ship noticed. There were no penetrators launched, no change of course, nothing. *Ottawa* didn't get word of their success until several hours after it was done, when the courier Blackfly made an early, unscheduled trip that initially had the CIC personnel wildly speculating as to what trouble they might be in. You should have seen the excitement and cheering when we heard the report—one seed ship tagged before it disappeared into the worm hole. They want to tag at least one more, so now we're just waiting for another to decide to leave the system. Then we're wrapping up and heading back home.

When I was younger, I read something in a book about the Native American tribes in the old settlement days. One of their supreme acts of bravery, more courageous even than killing a foe, was to touch them and then escape without harming them or getting harmed. They called it "counting coup". Well, we just counted coup on a Lanky seed ship, which makes those science nerds some of the bravest people in the entire Corps.

Love,
H.

August 10th, 2121
NACS *Ottawa*, Capella System

Andrew,

Happy anniversary, my love.

We've been married for nine years today. And what a nine years it has been. I don't think most marriages feature so much in the way of near death, mortal danger, and alien monsters. I do love to defy norms, you know. You know what I want for an anniversary present? Only for *Washington* to reappear.

Naturally, my thoughts are full of almost nothing but you today, no matter how hard I try to focus on other things. Remember getting engaged on Luna? I love how much I shocked you when I proposed we get hitched. You were expecting a breakup when I got serious about our relationship, and I watched your face go from crumpled to grinning and glowing. I will always treasure that memory. Of course, the fucking Fleet made us wait for 6 months to approve and actually get us our permission slip.

I still don't agree that marriage needs a "license." What is the requirement to get a marriage license? Classes? Direction in how to be married? Nope, just time enough for us to maybe die before we can lay claim to each others' pension. I don't know why the Fleet cares where that pension goes after the person who earned it is gone. I mean parents or spouse—what's really the difference to them? It still makes me a little mad that they—people we don't know and have never met and who will never meet or know us—have such power over our personal lives.

But I don't want to be angry today. I want to be happy thinking of you and our plans for our future. I know you wanted to get to a colony since you were young because you grew up in a PRC. And you know I had no such desire because I grew up middle class in TX. But then you discovered Liberty Falls and the Chief with your mom, and that's where I think we both want to be now. We are going to buy a house of our own and live happily ever after.

The thing we haven't figured out is if we plan to get jobs or make our own jobs like the chief has done. I still don't know what exactly I can do other than fly drop ships and

Dragonflies, but at least that knowledge would translate to the civilian world. But a civil pilot job would mean being gone a lot crossing the continent and the globe. I really have no idea what a combat controller can do in civilian life, but you do have your neural networks skills to fall back on, which is always a high-demand field. I just think you may hate being stuck to a desk. But who knows? Maybe you'll be ready for a low stress job by then.

I think I am getting there—the idea of having low stress, no personal mortal danger for me or being responsible for other people's lives is appealing in a way I never really considered. We have both just kept accepting greater and greater responsibilities with lives on the line beneath us without question. Well, I have, anyway—you were the one who started having reservations about it all years ago. But that's now how it's done in the Fleet or SpecOps. Pilots and podheads aren't supposed to ask too many questions or second-guess things. We are career track, and this is the career.

When you come back to me, we are going to have a long talk, I think. You know, we can always go to university. We both have the same amount of earned college hours we can build on.

I love you, Andrew, and your absence is physically painful in a way I still cannot describe with words. I need you back so we can get on with our lives, together.

Love,
H.

August 15th, 2121
NACS *Ottawa*, Capella System

Andrew,

They tagged another seed ship yesterday late during our watch cycle, but we didn't find out until early this morning. It was the same: no reaction, successful implantation.

My renewed and growing expectation is that *Washington* will be found—eventually—now that we have so many clues and will be getting more. The data we need to do that just has to be collected. My feelings are still mixed, though. I vacillate between hopeful and fearful, anxious and excited. I know that *Washington* has six months of provisions and that those can be stretched up to twice as long if you go all dried rations after all the fresh and frozen stuff is gone. That is always in the back of my mind and tempers my hope, the longer you're gone. It has been 169 days since *Washington* disappeared, closing in on six months. However, I also know all Avengers have the materials to construct green houses, so you could have rations even longer, and sustain yourselves. Beans are protein, after all, and they're not hard to grow. And water is everywhere in the universe, plus the ships can keep recycling water for a very long time without fretting it. The crew won't like it after a while, but it can be done. So, as I said, mixed feelings.

Right now, we're in Alcubierre heading back to Earth and riding high on the success of the bloodless mission. Both seed ships disappeared with an EM burst in the same spot. The scientists are excited, I can tell you. If this is where *Washington* left the system, we may very soon know where you went. Several new probes designed to read the trackers left in the seed ship hulls were left on station. That means battle groups will be returning every few months to gather the data the probes collect and maybe take out some more seed ships or tag more of them.

The science division released three Alcubierre-capable probes into the Lankies' wormhole three hours apart. If that's successful, we can create our own Alcubierre chute to that spot and either find you or open a way back for you. The caveat in this Alcubierre creation is that the probes have to come back before we can do anything because we don't know where this wormhole leads, so no triangulation points.

My hope is renewed, Andrew. Still, when you come home, we are absolutely having that conversation.When I get you back, I will have used up all my luck and then some, and I really don't want to have to roll those dice ever again because there'll be no way the universe would let them come up with a winning throw again.

Love,
H.

August 20th, 2121
Joint Base Burlington

Andrew,

I'm back on Earth, taking quasi-leave after that lengthy, boring, yet exciting mission to Capella. I just checked in at Burlington, where I'll be stationed for a few weeks working with a few pilots who are going on temporary loan to the Territorial Army.

Things are quiet with the Lankies right now. We're at a bit of a stalemate, from the looks of it. We haven't taken any colonies away from them, but they haven't taken any more. Rumor has it that we're going to start reconnoitering the systems the Lankies have taken, to look for evidence of more hidden wormholes.

Now that *Washington* has inadvertently discovered and revealed that anomaly in Capella, Astrophysics thinks that there must be more of them, which explains how they took over so much of our space so quickly and are so much more mobile between systems than we are. This last trip was such an eye-opener, both for us and the SRA. We've never seen Lankies use our Alcubierre chutes, though they obviously know where they are—you experienced their blockade in the Solar System at the Fomalhaut node personally, remember?

The biggest question of all is this: how the hell did they get into the Solar System the first time they showed up? No one saw them arrive before they hit Mars.

Anyway, there are probably dozens of missions coming up to all the colonial systems we've lost to do what *Ottawa* just did in Capella, but it will take longer because no other system has had a *Washington* incident to show the way. So we're not looking for fights yet, but we are looking for ways to get in planned rather than random fights that we can win and eject them from our systems. I do know the ultimate goal is to get rid of the Lankies and get our colonies back. Anyone with half a brain can figure that out. R&D and Science are the busiest divisions right now. They're pouring levels of funding into those branches they've never seen before. Maybe we should have done that from the start instead of just building more and bigger ships with more and bigger guns.

In the meantime, we have a lot of pilots in limbo, just waiting for the next move. The

TA asked to borrow pilots in a rotation to give their guys a break. They really hurt themselves when they exiled so many troops to Fomalhaut. As you can guess, that move didn't do much to recruit new bodies for the TA. Who wants to sign up for planetary defense and then get shipped off defending some colony? This group that I'm handing over volunteered for personal reasons for a three-month tour. Only one of these pilots is under my command. But I think Harris assigned me to the task because I told him how much good it did me to serve at Burlington last time.

    This is my second night in Burlington. This weekend, I'm heading to Chief Kopka's place.

    More soon.

    Love,
    H.

August 24th, 2121
Liberty Falls, VT

Andrew,

    I'm in Liberty Falls with the Chief. He hugged me fiercely when he saw me. It made me tear up and I got his shoulder wet. I fell right into helping him again and we've spent the entire weekend talking, with me filling him in on the new developments. I have never been at such peace, Andrew, as when I am idly chatting with him. With you, I am content and in love, but always rushed with our limited time between all the stress and excitement of our jobs; right now, with you MIA, I don't have you to share my life and days. The Chief knows you, so I have an ear that really hears me, like no one who doesn't know you can do. Right now, my peace is just being able to share my worries and my ideas. You are the only other person in my life I can do that with.
    It's different with the Chief, of course. He's content in his retirement, but speaks the military language—which is peacefully muted for him now. I do envy him. You and I were always so focused on each other when we had the rare leaves together that neither of us fully appreciated that about him. I'm seeing a whole new side of him, and it's filling a paternal hole in my life I didn't even know was there.
    Tomorrow will mark six months you've been absent from my life. The Chief and I talked about the food and water situation on the Avengers and he agrees that if you set up the green houses, you can stretch fresh food a lot longer. We know that crews can make the rations last for even longer if the ship needs to go lean. Plants would need water, of course, so you'd have to find a source, but that stuff is everywhere in the galaxy.
    I wish I could see where you are. My mind can't settle on a potential vision just because there are so many, many possibilities.

Love,
H.

August 25th, 2121
Joint Base Burlington

Andrew,

Today was a rough day.

Washington disappeared exactly six months ago. The Fleet changed the status of the ship from "Missing" to "Missing/Likely Lost." It's just one little change in the database, but it still hit me like a punch to the chest when I read it. I knew it was coming. The Chief and I talked about the fact that this is just a technical change, a deadline in place from colonization days, and probably not reflective of the modern reality of the concentrated nutrients we use today.

Still, those two words. I haven't given up on you, and I never will. But Fleet just took the first step toward officially writing you off. I am not prepared for the bereavement detail to show up at my door with a letter from Corps command and a box full of whatever personal stuff you left behind in Iceland. I know this is the half-way point, that one year is their magic line without any true evidence of loss. I truly never thought we would get here. In the beginning, I was sure you'd be long back by now.

You know that my conviction has been put to the test over the months, but the most recent discoveries have renewed my hope. Despite the potential ration and water situation, I know the engineering crews on the Avengers can work miracles. Survival is the greatest motivator of all. I'm pretty confident *Washington* will figure out how to keep feeding and watering the crew. And now that those wormhole probes are out there and seed ships are tagged, I have more hope we'll find you, or you'll come back before the year is up.

The CO called me to check on me, and I swear I almost cried. My voice was watery a few times during the conversation, and only my mortification at the thought of breaking down in front of him held me together. He could tell, though. He ordered me to take a couple of days off. I didn't argue with him this time.

I haven't had a proper drink in a while, mainly because I was worried that if I started to drown these worries with alcohol, I wouldn't stop. Tomorrow, I'll go back to the

Chief's place, but tonight, I think I'm headed to the O-Club here on base and I'm going to tell the orderly to make me a Shockfrost. I'll be thinking of you when I drink it, and hope you're out there somewhere, knocking back some awful illicit shipboard hooch distilled from kitchen recycler biomass.

    Love,
    H.

August 26th, 2121
Joint Base Burlington

Andrew,

I was so hungover this morning! The colonel doubtless suspected I wouldn't be up for work today. I decided to work it off, though, so I checked in with the Chief, packed some food and a sleeping roll, and took a hike up to our camping spot. The exercise was exactly what I needed. I'm still here, writing this entry outside, under the stars.

We always said we would see each other in these stars. It's a clear night, and I'm really lucky. A recent solar flare is bathing Earth in the aurora borealis tonight. That's hiding most of the stars, of course, but I'm taking that as a sign. I want to think the sky is in gorgeous, vibrant colors tonight because you're in a good place. I'm not giving up hope, Andrew. I'm not grieving. I took a picture of the sky to remind me in my gloomier days that you're still out there and are coming to back to me.

All my love, always,
H.

August 29th, 2121
Joint Base Burlington

Andrew,

I just got movement orders. I'm headed back to Goose Bay Monday. We're going back to Capella in a month for data retrieval and additional tagging. I'm excited about this because hope. *Ottawa* will be doing exactly the same thing—just about nothing. We can't risk stirring up the Lankies planet-side because we don't want to alert the seed ships something's going on in system, so the pilots are facing a fairly boring mission again if all goes according to plan. One of my best pilots is still embedded with the TA and they'll be there for a little while yet. She was supposed to be training new aircrews, but they have a shortage of pilots, so she's actually flying hot missions for them, dropping infantry platoons in PRC hot spots to reinforce the Lazarus Brigades whenever they need extra boots on the ground. I am worried about her—that shit can get as dangerous as going up against Lankies, as you well know.

I am actually glad to be assigned to a relatively peaceful situation in Capella. That's probably telling you just how much I have changed since *Washington* disappeared.

Love,
H.

September 3rd, 2121
Joint Base Goose Bay

Andrew,

One of my pilots died yesterday. She was 24 years old. She was the pilot we loaned to the TA. The drop ship she was flying went in and crashed while she was on a low-level training run.

I can't think of a worse way to go. Just a simple accident, snuffing out that young life. She wasn't married, and I wonder if she ever loved anyone. Now she'll never be married or get to enjoy the many years of life she should have had ahead of her. I wonder if she would have left in a few years or stayed in for years, like we have. I wonder if she ever would have had children. I wonder if she had a good relationship with her parents. I wonder, I wonder . . . But no one will ever know.

She didn't die under my command, so I wasn't responsible for making the call, but I did anyway. Her parents were really upset as you can imagine, but that doesn't mean she was on good terms with them. Mine would be upset, too, but I wouldn't care. I took them off my next-of-kin-to-be-notified list a long time ago. Today, I put Chief Kopka's name in that spot.

Her death has me thinking about us, about you. I have not regained my former excitement for the job, Andrew, though I am looking forward to the upcoming mission in a few weeks. The extent of that excitement is the chance of finding you. I already told you I am not even looking for ways to get behind the stick. I am thinking about the fact that I am still young enough to enjoy another life than the military life. But without you, I don't know what to do—not even what I <u>want</u> to do. My life has almost no frame of reference outside of the military. That's pretty fucking sad, isn't it? There's so much of life I haven't lived, <u>we</u> haven't lived, that I don't even know what I'm missing.

Sorry for the rambling thoughts, but I know you of all people will understand.

Love,
H.

September 15th, 2121
Liberty Falls, VT

Andrew,

I have been at the Chief's place for the last few days, just a quick leave before *Ottawa* leaves next week. There are some things I needed to sort out in my head, and I wanted to talk to him. I laced up my hiking boots and went up the mountain to our favorite spot day yesterday. I didn't stay out all night, though, not this time.

On the way here Friday night, I had an encounter on the train from the base back to Liberty Falls. There was an older guy in the compartment with me who started a conversation when he saw the uniform. Said I looked way too young to be a light colonel. He didn't believe me when I told him I'm in my mid-30s. He's a vet—said he served in the Marines before they became the Spaceborne Infantry. (He did not care for that name change, by the way.) I asked him a few questions to make sure he wasn't just some civvie bullshit artist, and he gave the right answers, so I think he was legit.

He told me something that has stuck with me ever since. He said he hardly ever sees people my age at his local vet chapter or at the VA. It's either older vets from the days before the Lankies, or young ones who joined after the Battle of Mars and left after their four-year term was up. The ones in between—that's us. The ones that enlisted right at the start of the Lanky war and fought through the worst of it, back before we had Orions and Avengers. They either didn't live long enough to become vets, or they're the old guard in the Corps now, the ones that pass on the hard lessons.

When I got home, I got curious and looked up our boot camp class in the database. Platoon 1066 had thirty-three recruits. Remember the first day at boot, when Sergeant Gau said maybe fifteen of us would finish our first term and muster out after four years? He was wrong in the end. Almost everyone died. We two are the only ones from our boot camp class assigned to the Fleet or the SI who are still alive. The others didn't even live through their first terms. They were just grist for the mill.

The Corps keeps records on everything. I did a little digging and put together my own statistics with the data from the personnel demographics database. Of all the Corps recruits of from our birth years who joined the same year we did, forty-six percent were killed in action in their first term. And that includes the TA troops, which skews the average because they have much lower casualty rates than the Fleet or the SI. It doesn't look much better for the five birth years that follow, either.

Of those from our generation who joined, half are dead. Most of the rest got out when they could.

Maybe that's why I've been feeling such a disconnect at work lately. I deal with colonels and generals who are ten or twenty years older, or junior officers and enlisted who are ten or fifteen years younger. There's hardly anyone left who's our age, who has seen what we've seen. That's why I don't hang out at the O-Club a lot. I can't relate to most of the other officers. The younger ones think I'm too serious and morose, and the older ones are in their own little rarified club, polishing each other's ribbon racks for networking and promotion points.

I don't know why I am telling you all of this. I guess I am mostly trying to let my head do that sorting out I mentioned. The world has changed around me, and maybe I need to change as well. Because right now, doing what I've always done, I am just holding on. And that's not good enough to get me through another seven years to retirement. But what would I do? Maybe it's stupid of me to even consider walking away, but then I think about how long a time seven years really is, and how much longer it will seem without you.

Love,
H.

September 25th, 2121
NACS *Ottawa*, Daedalus Station, Luna

Andrew,

We are easing away from Daedalus as I write, bound for data retrieval in Capella. I am shocked at how quickly they've mobilized *Ottawa* again. I've never seen the Fleet move this fast. We are escorting *Cincy* and *Nashville*, just like last time, with no other role to play than defense. This time, we are being joined by *Montevideo's* task force. She's another Class II Avenger. The highlight for my pilots and me will be courier duty, once again. The thrill of sneaking past Lankies does get the adrenaline pumping. I like doing it for the information I get to hear first hand and later relay to Command, so I'll be taking my runs when they come up in rotation. It turns out I really am looking forward to another Alcubierre transition. We're hitting the chute in about five hours.

Love,
H.

September 27th, 2121
NACS *Ottawa*, Capella System

Andrew,

Ottawa made it back to Capella System with some trouble this time.

There were two seed ships mid-system this time, loitering between the planet and their wormhole so we saw action almost immediately, much to the scientists' dismay. *Cincy* came in system yesterday and the Wonder Balls notified them to the presence of the seed ships. *Cincy* observed their pattern for half a day, then sent an Alcubierre probe to update *Ottawa* and *Montevideo*. The ships were projected to cross our path on the way to our destination, so *Ottawa* decided to take them out, prophylactically, with *Montevideo* making her first Lanky kill. We took the first shot with an Orion, aiming at Lima-1, but L-1 actually dodged the hit, like the one *Washington* pursued, then turned and came directly at us. You know they are far more nimble than we are, somehow, so we didn't think we could dodge it. And *Montevideo* had already targeted and released an Orion at Lima-2. They couldn't reposition or safely send an Orion or any other ordnance to assist.

Things were very dicey and CIC was in a near uproar with frantic, overlapping voices throwing out possible solutions. We thought the seed ship was working up to ramming speed. The best we thought we could do was use the particle cannons and hope to withstand the debris that would keep coming if we succeeded, but L-1 started to swing around to use its penetrators, depriving *Ottawa* the chance to use the warmed up particle mounts. The skipper ordered weapons to fire the A mount anyway while we still had a partial shot and we destroyed some of its aft portion. We got enough of it that it continued to spin away from us, spewing capsules and yellow-white fluids into space. But it was out of commission and we were able to keep going. It was at that moment that I realized how much I don't really enjoy danger anymore. I guess I am getting old, after all. That theme keeps resurfacing in the journal, doesn't it? Maybe I need to have that talk with myself, Andrew.

Science was pretty unhappy that they had two fewer seed ships in system to target for tagging. However, there are actually two more in orbit around Willoughby, so that helps a bit. I wonder what it is about this system that keeps them coming back in such numbers? On the other hand, we aren't monitoring any other systems yet, so maybe this is normal numbers and behavior. After we took care of the immediate threat, we made our way to the moons again and *Nashville* took up station near the wormhole. *Cincy* will patrol this time. I am itching to hear what the data from all those probes reveals.

    Love,
    H.

September 30th, 2121
NACS *Ottawa*, Capella System

Andrew,

I cheated a little on the courier rotation and put myself at the top of the list AND took shameless advantage of my rank to stay in CIC as much as I could. I stayed on *Cincy* for an entire watch before heading back to *Ottawa*.

Here are some of the things the data is telling us—two of the four the seed ships in Capella when we entered were detected coming into the system from their wormhole. Unfortunately, one of them destroyed two of the probes left to monitor the tagged ships if they come back. Luckily, we have some redundancy here, and there are two more probes scanning passively for the tags, and Engineering is working to add that ability to the Wonder Balls, as those are spread all over the system. Unfortunately, the passive scanning range is not great for the tags, only about three klicks. So far, there's no trace of a tagged seed ship. But everyone's excited because the software on the Wonder Ball probes is learning to detect seed ships better and better in the system, and it was able to isolate all four ships eventually. The AI built into them was able to individually ID the Lankies as they moved around the system. We now know that we killed the second and third to come through the wormhole since we left. This technology is incredible and pretty much lets us map the threats in-system without risk after they've been deployed.

The disappointing part is that there's no word of *Washington* yet. The other disappointment is that the probe Science sent into the wormhole that was set to return didn't make it back, but they have no idea why. Did it get destroyed because it wasn't designed for the wormhole? Is our Alcubierre technology incompatible with an existing wormhole—considering our drives make their own wormhole between specific points? Was it successful in getting through and then unable to return due to malfunction or destruction on the other end? We just don't know yet, and we may never find out. But they're working on new solutions to try with new probes even now.

Love,

H.

October 4th, 2121
NACS *Ottawa*, Capella System

Andrew,

The Lankies are really stirred up in Capella. I'm guessing it's because they know something took out two of their seed ships. They've changed their movement patterns, and now it looks like they're on the prowl, trying to sniff out whatever is cutting down their numbers all of a sudden. We had to play hide-and-seek with them for a while, and it felt too much like the old days when we were constantly on the defensive. We could go head-to-head and just wipe them out with our combined combat loads of Orions, but that would fuck the scientific mission and leave nothing behind to study and track, so we are playing chicken instead.

It feels like every time we come up with gear or tactics to stay ahead of them, they pull even with us eventually, and I hope that our advantage this time will hold long enough for us to find *Washington* and bring you home because I'm not prepared to consider the alternative.

Love,

H.

October 7th, 2121
NACS *Ottawa*, Capella System

Andrew,

We lost a courier today. He was one of my drop ship jocks, 1LT Newport. He was a happy person, one of those people you just love having in your squadron—always so positive, funny, and committed to his job. His Dragonfly hit an undetected mine and just disintegrated. He was on the path between *Cincy* and *Ottawa*, the same path I've traveled several times now. We don't know where it came from. Are they just drifting in the system, invisible to us? Drawn to the lesser gravity of the ships or the wormhole? Whatever it was, another precious life is gone, another life mostly unlived, thanks to these creatures.

Andrew, I am so tired of this. On days like today, I hate sitting in the squadron CO's chair. We've both lost people under our command, but I don't know how many more I-regret-to-inform-you messages I can write to next of kin before I lose my shit. How much longer do I hold off on living my own life? As I said, things are still not sorted out in my head. I think they're getting more jumbled, actually.

Where are you, Andrew? When are you coming back to me? We have lives to live and we're supposed to live them together.

Love,
H.

October 10th, 2121
NACS *Ottawa*, Capella System

Andrew,

Yesterday, *Cincy* tagged another seed ship exiting the system via the wormhole, so now there are three out there in the universe somewhere. Not twelve hours later, another ship came back into the system—not a tagged ship, but a new one. It set off all kinds of alarms, but it was detected instantly and *Cincy* got some new EM data from the entry, though I don't know if it's any different from the exit EM noise. Still, more data is good data. But there are three ships in system again. Is that a special number for them? There were four when we arrived. There's so much we don't know.

We have decided to wrap up this mission before we have more casualties. Science managed to send a probe into the wormhole on the heels of the Lanky they tagged, which was a first. Of course, they have no idea how long it will be before it's back, if ever. The previous probes haven't returned yet, so we're no closer to setting up a new Alcubierre node to wherever you went. Regardless of any of that, the system is getting hot again, and this task force isn't here for a fight. We leave in eight hours while the path to the chute is clear.

Love,

H.

October 11th, 2121
NACS *Ottawa*, Solar System

Andrew,

We made it back to the Solar System. I told you Capella was getting hot, and I think we left just in time. Two of the seed ships broke orbit around Willoughby as we were making our way to the Alcubierre node, heading in the same direction. We don't know if they were going for us or if they are just going to take up station at our node, or something else entirely, but we all felt intense relief when we felt ourselves in Alcubierre, despite the usual discomfort. I have never entered Alcubierre with something in pursuit of my ship before and I can say for sure that the sense of relief as we escaped into the chute completely overrode the discomfort I felt.

I am looking forward to some down time when I get back to Earth. I am certain the CO will grant me as much leave as I want. I haven't really taken advantage of his offer yet, but I think it's high time. I keep having these dreams where we come through the Capella chute, and there's a fleet of a hundred of the bastards waiting for us, ready to pounce.

Love,
H.

October 31st, 2121
Liberty Falls, VT

Andrew,

I am feeling good today, for the first time in a while.

I'm on a three-day special leave because you are still missing and my CO is a pretty great guy. He classified it as "bereavement" leave, though I haven't given up on you.

I am very worried about you and *Washington's* ability to hold out and survive. These Avengers are not built to stay out for that long without resupply or maintenance. But three days will not change the worry and anxiety I am feeling. Only you getting back to Earth will change that.

I did the hike to our spot yesterday, up the mountain and along the ridge. It's late October, and fall is over. I missed the best of it while I was in Capella, but I can smell and see the aftermath. The ground is covered with yellow and red leaves that give off that scent when I walk through them. Some are already brown, but most are still vibrant. The only advantage of my timing is that the leaf-peepers have already come and gone from Liberty Falls. The Chief's place is back to mostly local traffic.

When the sun started to set yesterday, I was still up there. The sky was mostly clear, and I could see the stars popping out as I sat there in the gathering darkness. I had my sleeping bag and mat with me, so I decided to stay out all night under those stars. I don't even know if you're in a place that can be seen from the northern hemisphere, but it made me feel closer to you anyway. Wherever you are, you're still a part of the universe, and I wanted to take it all in without a ceiling over my head to block the view. We always said we would meet each other in the stars if we lost each other. Are you near one of those stars, Andrew? Which one? Remember that night we spent painstakingly locating the star systems where we have colonies? I suppose it's possible the Lankies have wormholes that crisscross our colony systems, so maybe you're in one of them. That's not much of a comfort, considering how many we have lost to the Lankies, but we know now that we really can sneak around with an Avenger in a Lanky system, and I'm sure you'd be doing exactly that if that's where you are. That is a bit of comfort, actually.

Chief Kopka is always happy when I visit, but I could see sorrow in his eyes. Both worrying and supporting someone else in their worry is a burden, but it is also a burden shared, so I think that makes it better for both of us. We owe him so much for his kindness over the years. I am so happy that my relationship with him has moved beyond friends and acquaintances to the point that he is kind of a replacement father—one I chose because he is worthy of the title, and because he thinks you and I are worthy, too.

He asked me about my parents today. He remembered that I had a falling out with them, but I never told him the sordid details before, so we had a long talk on the subject. He said that eight years is a long time to hold a grudge, and that maybe I should consider reaching out to them, especially now.

I'm sure my mother would be happy to see me return to the family fold without you. She'd treat me like a wounded bird, act like she's patching me up, and then put me on the shelf so her friends can admire what a good job she did with me, and how selfless and caring she is. All the blame for our long silence would fall on you. But I can't forgive her for the cardinal sin she committed, when she tried to turn me against you. We were already married! I had made my choice and she didn't respect that. She could have simply kept that to herself, but when she tried to physically drive a good-looking male wedge between us, you know I had no choice. My anger would not be contained—I didn't even try to contain it. Gods, it gets my blood pressure up even now. No, I have no desire to see her or even talk to her.

So I won't be going down to San Antonio any time soon. They're not my family anymore, you are. You, the Chief, and that little cluster of cells in the freezer at that reproductive clinic, the one that carries both our DNA. I'll never get permission to use it while I am in the Corps, but it's comforting to know that it's there, a part of you and me that will survive us both.

I think I'll go up to our spot again tonight. There's just enough daylight left for me to make the climb. I'll meet you in the stars tonight, all right?

Love,

H.

November 2nd, 2121
Liberty Falls, VT

Andrew,

You know that old saw about the relative nature of time—it goes by in a hurry when you're doing something fun, and it slows to a crawl when you're sitting in a boring staff meeting or working out in the gym. Well, I think I've uncovered another paradox like that.

Every day at work is an interminable drag right now that feels like a week and a half of hours, whether I'm sitting behind a desk or in a cockpit. And yet, somehow it's already been over three months since we went to Capella to find *Washington* the first time and we've been back another two times since then, which is an insanely intense deployment tempo for the Fleet. It's the worst of everything—days that won't end, and months that fly by.

You know I'm always sad to see the end of fall around here, when the leaves are spent and everything is just brown, and the days turn from pleasantly crisp to that shitty combination of wet and cold that leeches the warmth right out of your body. This year, it was especially depressing because we missed all the beauty that came before it, the best three or four weeks of the year. October was always our time here—the fall colors, the hikes, the hot mulled cider and wine at the Chief's place. It was the fuel that got me through all those deployments without you. This visit, neither of us got to see any of it. I feel like I just wrote this, but these thoughts are heavy on me. Fall will come again, just like you will come back to me. It's just a matter of time. And there's so much time ahead of us.

I don't know who said it, but I read a quote once about grief and joy—that grief can take care of itself, but to get the full measure of joy, you need to have someone to share it with. That's only half the truth for me so far. My joys are diminished without you to share them, that's for damn sure. And "grief" needs to be replaced with "worry" for this to apply to me. My worry hasn't diminished yet, not even a little, and it keeps growing the longer you're out there. My life with you had all the colors of the fall and that aurora borealis. Without you here, it's as drab and cold as the weather outside, and everything is the same shade of brown.

But I am letting myself get too gloomy now. I blame the stupid weather. It's a few months of cold and early darkness, but the leaves will pop out all new and green in the spring again, and we'll be hiking through the fall foliage together again next year. I'm reporting back to Goose Bay tomorrow. I will miss the freedom of no one to order about or to be ordered about by someone else.

Love,
H.

November 8th, 2121
Joint Base Goose Bay

Andrew,

Today is my 35th birthday. No one here knows unless they happen to look it up, and I'm not volunteering that info. The truth is that I don't much feel like celebrating without you. My worry over your absence consumes me. I'm not worried that you're dead, but I am worried that you will be. My brain just won't stop calculating the calories, the crew complement, the fuel, and so on. And the truth is that there may be no problem with any of that at all. I just have no way of knowing. Perhaps you found another Arcadia on the other side of that worm hole and have all the resources you need, but your Alcubierre drive needs repair, and engineering is even now manufacturing a new part. If my brain would dwell on the positive possibilities, I would be so grateful. Instead. . . (Can you hear the heavy sigh I just wrote into that word? My brain is my worst enemy right now, I think.)

Today was just a day of routine technical training in the classroom. I'm done this so many times, I was on autopilot, not even thinking too much about what I was saying. It was like I turned on a pre-recorded lecture I stored in my brain years ago. So much so that I don't recall any salient moments from the class at all.

When I got back to our quarters, I played your suit telemetry again. Hearing your voice is like a birthday present from you. I relish the surety, the confidence, and the competence in the words you use and the tone of your voice, especially under pressure, and my impressions are reinforced by the responses you get from your team. My favorite part, the part I just can't hear enough, is that exchange with Elin after your bird went down on Willoughby (also the one on the drop to the planet). She's funny. I can't wait to meet her when you get back.

Love,
H.

November 30th, 2121
Joint Base Goose Bay

Andrew,

It's been a while since I needed to write to you, which is what this journal is supposed to be doing for me, I suppose.

I write when I need to write, when you just take over my mind with any emotion and I can't do anything else. The Fleet shrink said that's exactly what he had in mind when he assigned it. In general, I think he was right. It really does work. As long as I keep writing to you, you exist and it is just a matter of time before you come back to me. That may not be what the shrink intended, but that is what I've made this, and it absolutely works for me. I know you'll read these pages one day, and that keeps me going.

I just don't know how much longer I will keep going with the Fleet. That is an unintended side-effect of this journal, one that I doubt the shrink ever saw coming. It has made me think a lot about me, my job, and our future, and I just don't know that future is still with the Fleet. I'm still thinking of our zygote (what an ugly name!) that now needs a womb to continue to grow. Who will carry it in the future if I don't? I have the required womb, but am I'm approaching the time when it won't be viable anymore. If someone else does carry it in the future, they will know nothing of us or the reason we created it in the first place. The reason for its existence will be gone. That's just one more thing in my head and on my conscience at the moment. That zygote is a part of you.

If I decide to carry it, does that mean I'm admitting you're dead?

Is there really a difference between not believing you're dead, and not wanting to believe it?

If I use the embryo that we created as a fail-safe for each other, does that mean I accept you are gone for good?

I don't want that, Andrew. But I think if I don't carry our child, no one else will. A pregnancy changes everything for me. I won't be able to keep my position with the Fleet. If I had a higher rank, then I probably could, but I still have to ship out and enter

Alcubierre. I don't know what that does to pregnancies. Does anyone? I've got to do some research.

    Love,
    H.

December 5th, 2121
Joint Base Goose Bay

Andrew,

The answer is that no one knows what going through Alcubierre does to a pregnancy, not really. The only people likely to go through Alcubierre pregnant are colonists, but my Science division friend Evelyn says there have been no studies on this, and no one has ever followed the colonists to study Alcubierre effects after they reached their colonies. Livestock embryos are sent through Alcubierre frozen and they don't appear to suffer in that state, or biology would have heard about the loss of very important colony resources. But a gestating embryo is a total unknown. I don't want to be a test case. Plus, can you imagine me trying to fit in a flight suit pregnant? The image makes me laugh.

Love,
H.

December 25th, 2121
Liberty Falls, VT

Andrew,

I had a plan to avoid my first Christmas without you, but my XO thoroughly foiled it by taking the watch officer shift in my stead tonight. He thinks he is doing me a favor. I know he's in boiling hot water with his husband because of that decision—so I expressed my gratitude, let it stand, and went home to our little pad.

When I got home, Chief Kopka invited me to dinner in his quarters on short notice. I didn't want to be rude, so I accepted even though I wasn't really feeling that holiday spirit. Now I am back upstairs after a nice dinner with the chief and his new girlfriend, and I don't have to feel like a third wheel anymore. Her name is Selena, and she is very nice, but she is not a veteran, so most of our military shop talk went right over her head.

I know we never really cared about Christmas as a religious holiday, and we've spent plenty of them apart over the years because one of us was out on deployment. Still, this one is hitting me a little differently than the other solitary ones. It's a terrible thing to say, but it almost makes me wish we had a war going on right now. I don't want to say that out loud because the universe may grant me my wish and materialize another Lanky incursion on Greenland or something equally delightful. So I'm accepting my current fate and staying holed up in our apartment with a blanket on my lap, a mug of mulled wine on the table in front of me, your mom's rosary beads in my hand, and some old holiday vids on the network screen.

I don't want to whine too much. I'm warm and comfortable, and I've had a good meal with the Chief and Selena. I'm guessing that I'm almost certainly more safe and comfortable than you are right now, wherever and however you're spending this evening. But if I could drop everything and push a button to be there with you, I would do it in a heartbeat, without a second thought.

Love,

H.

January 1st, 2122
Joint Base Goose Bay

Andrew,

It's a new year, the next one on the calendar since *Washington* disappeared.

I am still not ready to give up on you, but I am thinking more and more about that frozen-in-time life we created. We made it as a sort of backup for each other, so we would have a piece of the other if something went wrong and one of us was lost. In hindsight, I don't know how logical that was for you, as you don't have a womb and would have to find someone to carry it to term. For me, on me other hand, it is still a possibility, but not for too much longer.

I keep returning to this theme—I am getting older, my body is not that young anymore. If I want this fail-safe to materialize, I am the only one who can make it happen.

I do wish your mother was still here. I could really use the maternal advice she would have given me. Your mom was a true mother. She cared about you and respected or at least went along with the choices you made without complaint or condemnation. It's so much more than I can say for my parents. You know my father has reached out over the years and I have given him the bare minimum. I wonder if I have short-changed him. He is a weak person, under the thrall of my mother, who does despicable things. But I wonder if he is really hurting, unable to free himself from her for some reason, and I never appreciated that fact over the years. He loved me and was a far more affectionate parent than she was. She was only ever interested in her social standing. You know that he has reached out to me via Milnet over the years. If I let him come back into my life, I don't have to let her come back into my life as well. He and the Chief would have nothing in common, but should I let that be a deciding factor? Just thinking out loud, or silently, on a screen here, I guess.

On base, people are celebrating the New Year, as always. I've gone to our quarters to think. I'm not much in the mood for celebrating. I want more answers from the Capella system, but I can only wait. I do get news occasionally. I made friends with one of the scientists, Evelyn Green. She and I exchange messages often. She always passes on anything new when she can. She's the one who told me there are no studies on the effect of Alcubierre on embryos in gestation. We bonded over the missing *Washington* because she's friends with the funny Elin Vandenberg who's on board with you. Apparently, Vandenberg is brilliant when it comes to synthesizing data on Lankies and intuiting their nature and their biology. Evelyn misses Elin, who was kind of a big-sister mentor. I guess she's a really big deal in the science division. She's actually the lead xenobiologist for the NAC Science Corps, but you probably know that by now.

Evelyn knows I am missing you, so we commiserate a bunch. It's actually really nice to have someone to worry with. I showed her your suit telemetry from Willoughby and she was utterly amazed at the footage as a scientist, and laughed at your interactions with Elin, as I do. Your confidence about survival gives both of us hope. And I just love to hear your voice.

I watch your last message to me all the time—before you entered Alcubierre Capella, when you couldn't reveal your destination but told me obliquely. Gods, I miss you! I miss us, Andrew. I miss our Haldrew speak, as you have dubbed it, our special patois that grew from shared experience, references only the two of us would get. That message has plenty of Haldrew speak, and I love it. That's also the most recent image I have of you, and I just like to look at you.

Love,
H.

January 31st, 2122
Liberty Falls, VT

Andrew,

I'm visiting the Chief for the weekend. I got in early enough today to help him out in the restaurant and I realize that like it. I know that will shock you. It shocked me, too. I think I like it because it is so different from my regular job, which is mostly repetitious right now, training again and again, and again, sending my pilots to Mars for planetary training; my job just keeps going in circles and I expect it will be like this until my next promotion. I'm just putting in time. As simple as helping out here is, it's new and new always appeals.

Ottawa is still in a holding pattern, awaiting movement orders and a mission. *Wellington* finally might be ready for action. She was sent out on a test run to Arcadia a few days ago, and I'll hear the results when I get back. That would give us two Avengers again, at least until the Pacific Alliance has its legs fully under it and all their ships are online. But that's not enough with the plans Fleet is making to reconnoiter our former colonies, so they have commissioned two more ships to be built at Daedalus. We need as many of them as they can put together. The future is going to require more joint missions with the South Americans, Euros, and SRA, all of whom have Avengers. I suspect NAC will be paying them with future resources from our colonies if we can manage to get them back. I also think there are going to be shifting alliances between all the blocs with Avengers to help each other out. Things continue to change on Earth politically. If only we'd had all this international camaraderie before the Lankies came calling. Life would be so different on Earth right now.

Love,
H.

February 13th, 2122
Joint Base Goose Bay

Andrew,

Happy 36th Birthday!

I wish we were together today. That isn't new. I wish we were together any day, everyday. Andrew, I hope you are having a good day, wherever you are. I am still waiting for you.

All is quiet and on hold with *Ottawa*. The Fleet is planning some recovery actions in the future, though details are murky, but I know it will begin with system surveillance like we have done at Willoughby. I think they'll be focusing on non-nuked planets first, and those with the shortest Lanky occupation. The idea is that we think can figure out their patterns and their entry point, get into system and clear it out, then start to retake our colonies. We're assuming now that every system they've taken might have a worm hole entry previously undetected by us. And that they don't have worm holes in the systems they haven't taken, of course. The worm holes are clearly their version of Alcubierre. The difference is that their worm holes appear to be two-way streets, based on what we discovered in Capella.

If it's two-way, how do they avoid collisions? Do they have the equivalent of air traffic controllers? How do they make their worm holes? So many unknowns, but it is utterly fascinating.

How the hell did *Washington* use their chute? And where does it lead? Best guess is their home system, but it could be to one of ours, too. How long can you survive in a place lousy with Lankies in space? Alone? Without food, fuel, and weapons resupply? At six months, you would have run out of fresh and frozen food and moved to rations, which would have lasted another six months if you made them stretch. There is the complete unknown of hydroponics on shipboard or resupply from planets in a Lanky system that certainly have water, but the food is a total unknown. We've only been back to one planet where they've had years to entrench. I personally saw how the vegetation exploded on Willoughby under their care, and your suit telemetry revealed that at Willoughby City, but can you eat it? And will they let you land? You can't refuel on their planets, so that would be tricky at best.

    I'm going down a dark path with these thoughts, so I'll stop that shit right now. *Washington* will figure out how to survive. That ship has a lot of resources on board and a lot of smart people motivated to survive.

    How will you do it? It's a mystery. You'll reveal everything when you come home, and I can't wait to hear it all.

    Love,
    H.

February 18th, 2122
Joint Base Goose Bay

Andrew,

I was feeling very maudlin about your absence after your birthday, which made me think about how about how my father must feel. But I'm here on Earth, so contact is still possible. I thought of the tragedy he would feel if I were to disappear without a trace and put myself in his shoes.

Then I did something that may shock you. I started to forgive him—a little. I reached out to him to ask how he is doing. Here's what he wrote back:

My dearest Di,

I could not have been more pleased to hear from you, it absolutely made my day, week, and month, certainly it is the highlight of the new year!

I'm doing well—still in my same R&D position. I should already be retired, but I've put it off because I don't really know what else I would be doing. Your mother still loves to entertain, of course, but that's not much fun for me, as you know. I don't want that to be how I am forced to spend the majority of my time, just because I'm available. And I like my work. I like to know that I am helping people like you (and Andrew) out, maybe keeping you safe out there. That is what drives me and keeps me engaged.

I'm physically okay, but I'm not really happy at home, outside of work. I miss your energy and your presence in my life, Diana. You are the best thing that came out of my marriage to your mother. I know you want nothing to do with her, so I will respect that and not share our communications, in case that worries you or is in any way a barrier to you continuing to talk to me. I would dearly love to see your beautiful face again. Would you consider coming out to see me? Or could I come see you, maybe? Let me know if I am overstepping.

Love, Dad

It looks like I may have opened a can of worms with my message to him, but what's done is done. Now I'm a little torn. What do I really want out of this?

I think it's because I'm feeling hollow with your absence and all the worry that comes with that. I don't think I'm ready for the next step with Dad so soon. I'm not excited about seeing him again—after all, it's not him I really want to see. But I've started something here, so do I go see him? I have zero desire to ever go to San Antonio again. Maybe I'll offer to meet him somewhere else, maybe in Burlington, on neutral ground. Having him come here and meet the Chief is like really letting him into my life again, and I am not quite prepared to do that yet.

Oh, decisions, decisions. More about this later.

Love always,
H.

February 25th, 2122
Joint Base Goose Bay

Andrew,

It has been a year since you disappeared. Today, *Washington's* status changed from Missing/Presumed Lost to Lost in Action. The gut punch I felt six months ago is nothing compared to today. Fleet wasted no time sending your effects from Iceland, and I'm looking at the box now. I'm not going to unpack it. You'll probably want to put all that stuff in your new office when you get back.

I know we did important things—that we saved lives, maybe even the entire planet. And yes, we got medals and fast promotions for doing all that. But I've never let any of that fool me into thinking the Fleet considered us special. Those medals were as much morale boosters for the rest of the Corps as they were recognition for us. In the end, we're all disposable, just an entry in a database someone's going to flip from "missing/presumed lost" to "Deceased" sooner or later without feeling any sorrow or grief. It's literally just a matter of time.

This may sound like I am bitter or angry, but I'm not. We've all known it from the day we came back from our first combat deployment, whether we admitted it to ourselves or not. When you're young, you just think you're the exception, that lightning will strike others but never you.

Maybe that's why they discourage marriage between Corps members. They don't want that lightning strike to take two people out of the fight—the one who gets struck and the one who has to live with the aftermath. But we did it anyway, and I'm not sorry. You are the best thing in my life, the only thing in my life that makes it worth living. The Fleet simply had to change your status because an administrative timeline was crossed, not because it's actually true. There's no ship, no body, no proof you're gone. I will never stop believing that you are still alive and out there somewhere. I know with total certainty that you are doing everything you can to make your way back to me. Because I would do the same in your place--and fuck the Fates.

Love,
H.

March 3rd, 2122
Ottawa, Daedalus Station, Luna

Andrew,

Wellington came limping back from her mission to Arcadia today, a month overdue. She experienced Alcubierre drive loss when she transitioned back into the Solar System and was apparently lucky to get here at all. That's every ship's nightmare—to be lost forever in the chute. So it's back to the shipyard with her. I'm glad I'm not on the PacAlliance engineering team, I can tell you that. Heads are going to roll over this one. The amount of money put into that ship could have built two more already.

There are two Flight III Avengers under construction now, but they're not ready yet, so we're doing a joint task mission with *Berlin* again. (At least the Germans know how to build a working ship.) This time we're going to 51 Pegasi. It just so happens that that planet was one of the better producers of the ore we need for ships. Coincidence? Definitely not.

We leave in a week. I've got a new crop of students full of bravado, piss, and vinegar that I've got to drain from them—again. Some of them will be going on this mission, so my days are jam-packed until we leave. You know what I'll be doing!

Love,
H.

March 10th, 2122

Ottawa, 51 Pegasi System

Andrew,

We've arrived in system with our task force of two Cincinnati class ships, *Chicago* and *Atlanta*. *Berlin* is also with us with her own little battle group, including their version of a stealth ship. This is her task force's maiden voyage out of the Sol System. They've got their own variety of surveillance probes they are deploying, but they are tied into our network so any NAC ship can retrieve data from their probes, and vice versa. Our task here is going take at least a few weeks and possibly months waiting and watching for seed ship activity. We're starting from scratch in this system, so we have no hard data whatsoever about numbers, mines, worm holes, etc. It's going to be a long slog, but we've got plenty of supplies.

As per protocol, *Atlanta* and *Chicago* went in first to scout. Just like when you returned to Capella last year, the system appears to be largely empty of seed ships at first glance, but it's pretty hard to spot them right off and under EMCON.

Science now has a pattern for two occupied systems (just a preliminary pattern for this one, of course), but they now believe the Lankies can identify our entry points and understand the quickest route we will take to the colonies. They think this system isn't as heavily mined or monitored because we haven't been back at all since it was taken.

Our objective is the same as yours initially in Capella. We assess the situation, proceed at *Ottawa's* skipper's discretion regarding the NAC planet, but we will also deploy Wonder Balls and search for a wormhole entry. We have discussed the possibility of a retrieval mission like you did on Willoughby, getting the data modules from the main Admin building, but there's no hard decision on that yet; the risk is that we will stir them up too much for Science to do their thing right now. Evelyn says she would love to get on the planet to get samples and compare it to Willoughby. In the meantime, we're still trying to spot Lankies in the system. There were two mining colonies here, so this system would be a great one to reclaim. I only remember you've been to this system because you mentioned it in a message to me that I recently reread.

That was when the SRA and NAC were still ignoring the common threat to Earth. You were commenting on the tragedy of us killing each other, as if we hadn't just lost Willoughby to the Lankies.

I haven't been to this system before, but I have been to many others just like it. My Science friend, Evelyn, is on *Atlanta*, but it hasn't taken up any sort of station yet. *Atlanta* and *Chicago* are quietly looping the system, looking for Lanky seed ships and any sign of sudden EM bursts. For now, the ships are communicating via tight beam, but once they find the sweet spot, we won't risk even tight beams so they can tag more Lankies without interference. The Euros are doing the same with their task force. Maybe we won't be here for months, with two teams working toward the same goal. I really, really don't want to be here that long.

Love,
H.

March 12th, 2122
Ottawa, 51 Pegasi System

Andrew,

This mission may not take as long as I had feared at first. The Euro stealth ship *Temeraire* identified two seed ships orbiting Pegasus a, and the Wonder Balls identified a third circling the SRA moon. That makes three in system again, which does seem to be a pattern. But should it be four, like in Willoughby? Are the numbers per system or per planetary body? Will a fourth one show up and reveal their wormhole? Or were there four in Capella only because we had stirred them up and they called in reinforcements? If so, how?

The xenoscience is really intriguing me. It makes me wonder about a career change. Of course, that would mean years of university. How much time do I have left to even consider stuff like that? Like you, I already have a couple of years under my belt, back from before I opted to enlist. That was when I had no idea whatsoever about what I was interested in studying or doing for a career. I think I have enough of the basic courses to be able to launch into focused studies if I decide to go that route. It's been a long while, though—can you even imagine us back in school, after everything we've been through, sitting and taking notes among a bunch of zit-faced kids half our age? Still, I will check on my existing credits, just in case.

I'm still thinking of that lonely embryo in cryo that's waiting for one of us to reclaim it. That would definitely preclude years of university, wouldn't it? Still, it's the science and the search for answers that has me engaged the most these days. Particularly now, when my pilots and I have zip to do. Regardless, I can't deny that I'm changing. I've lost that thing that makes us take mortal risks without a second thought. I think that thing is called "youth." Now there's a thought that's comforting and depressing at the same time.

It's hard to write a chuckle into words in a journal, but that was a chuckle.

Love,
H.

March 13th, 2122
Ottawa, 51 Pegasi System

Andrew,

This system just got hot. We lost *Atlanta* today. One of the seed ships on station around Pegasus ac left its orbit without the Wonder Balls catching on and fired penetrators at her. Command is still trying to figure out how the seed ship detected *Atlanta*, which was running with tight EMCON. They were drifting between moons while looking for that wormhole and (I thought) watching the seed ships. We may never know, though. Some personnel managed to get into the escape pods— only three out of the twenty-eight available pods, and they had to be retrieved planet-side because of the trajectory the computer chose to send the pods. The computer just calculated a path away from the destruction, but it did not take into account the danger of the other seed ship in orbit. Overall, it was just a clusterfuck of errors.

I scrambled my team and the SAR birds and we dropped to the surface with four Dragonflies each escorting the 3 SAR birds. I was hoping with everything I had that Evelyn was on one of those pods. She wasn't. Pegasus ac has the same flying conditions you experienced at Willoughby and New Svalbard, the same as on every Lanky-claimed colony we know of so far: turbulent, rainy, cloudy, dangerous with lightning. The one thing the computer did right, though, was to get the pods to land near each other. It was a still a bitch of a rescue. Two landed in a river below a spit of land the third landed on. The two in the water were quickly carried downstream, but at least they were together, so two SAR birds pursued them and I played escort to them while the 3rd SAR group recovered the other pod and got off planet. All the while the pods were shrieking SOS, just grating on all our nerves, knowing we were certainly going to be in a fight with Lankies. However, the river proved helpful in that respect only because it moved the pods away faster than the Lankies could pursue.

We had to wait until the pods got trapped in a sandy bend of the river to land. The Lankies were slow to catch up, and we were able to gun them all down before they could reach the site, but my flight fired pretty much every missile and cannon shell we had.

The last ones dropped just a few hundred meters short of the pods.

One of our ships put down, and the Spaceborne Rescue team retrieved the pod passengers. The end result is another kick in my stomach, Andrew. One pod had a hatch seal breach, and everyone inside drowned.

My friend Evelyn is gone. She didn't even make the pods, and I am feeling the deepest sense of bereavement I have ever felt. I have been sobbing, open-mouthed, snot and saliva all over.

I haven't had a real friend other than you in years. Well, I have the Chief, and I love him, too, but he's more like a father figure than a friend to make plans with and laugh. Evelyn was also a connection to you, however distant, and the one other person who had a stake in *Washington's* survival, who believed with me that you're still out there. I didn't realize how much I needed that until it was gone. No more funny messages back and forth, no more supportive vid calls, no more anything. Just gone, with so much stuff unsaid and undone.

My soul is wearing thin, Andrew. I feel wrung out. I have been kicking around the idea of resigning for a while. I talked to Evelyn about it a lot. She wasn't in a combat occupational specialty, of course, so she couldn't quite understand the burden that goes with that, but she listened to me, and she empathized. I'm going to miss her so much.

Gods, I need you back. I need you in my life. I need to talk to you.

Until recently, the thought would have felt a little like heresy, but I think I'm finally done with the Fleet. When we get back, I'm going to resign my commission.

The thought of dying bothers me, but not because I'm afraid of death. For me, it would just be over. What bothers me is the grief I'd leave in my wake for the Chief, and the oblivion that would await the embryo. Without me, it will get trashed and you and I —we—will be gone forever. And if I'm gone when you get back, Andrew... I just don't want that to happen to you.

Love,
H.

March 15th, 2122
Ottawa, Solar System

Andrew,

We're back in our own system. The Lankies were all stirred up after the action in 51 Pegasi, and the skippers decided the Wonder Ball deployment was enough for now. They'll be gathering data that some other task force will have to retrieve in the future. I spent the time in Alcubierre, hopefully my last time in Alcubierre, drafting my resignation letter and preparing my application to get impregnated with our embryo. I won't send the application until my resignation is registered and accepted. I'll be six years shy of full retirement, but I'll have decent retirement and all our savings we have amassed over the years. Now that I've made the decision, I feel somewhat revived, and relieved that you won't come home to find me gone as well.

Evelyn's death pushed me over the edge. It is still so visceral, and I tend to break down into tears easily whenever I think about it. I thought about the fact that I have absolutely no career in the civilian world, that I have no idea what I'm going to do to manage being pregnant or what I'm going to do when the baby comes. The first person I'm checking in with is the Chief, maybe before I submit this resignation. I know I should think this through from all angles, and he can help me do that from a different headspace. But Andrew, I am so tired, so lost without you. I don't know how I can go on in the Fleet with nothing to look forward to, no one else to commiserate with, and constantly feel the lack of your presence. I need purpose and that piece of us in cryo was put there for this very reason. We have to go on and that bundle of cells will allow us to do just that.

Love,
H.

March 20th, 2122
Liberty Falls, VT

Andrew,

Happy Spring Equinox!

Outside, the trees are just starting to show the tiniest pops of green as their leaves are thinking about unfurling. There's still quite a bit a snow, as always this time of year, and the patches of ground in town are all muddy with melt. This isn't my favorite time of year here, as you know. No hiking, no staying outside. But in a few months, everything will be green and blooming. I just have to wait. I've gotten pretty good at waiting now; I've been waiting on you for over a year. I wish you would hurry up and get back already!

I'm at the Chief's place and it's about 0300. I'm in our rooms holding your mom's rosary beads. The Chief and I have been talking for hours. The first thing I said to him when I arrived was "I need to talk." I'm sure I was quite a sight with my snotty nose and my red eyes. He immediately hugged me and said we would talk as long as I needed after we had privacy after closing. I arrived during the dinner hours, so I pitched in and helped serve, chop, wash, bus, and cash out.

After the doors were locked, I asked him, "How would you like to be grandfather?", and you should have seen the smile that appeared—instantly. He said he would be honored to be thought of as a grandfather to our child. And then we were talking while we cleaned, prepped for the morning menu, scrubbed the floors, and set the tables. Afterward, he poured drinks for us. Not Shockfrosts, just mulled red wine. It is pretty cold tonight, around -7 Celsius, so it was a perfect choice. We sat in the living room in his place and talked and talked and talked. I told him about Evelyn, about the Fleet declaring you dead, about my diminished interest in my job. He knew about the Fleet declaration already, of course, but Evelyn's death and the fact that I can't find purpose or joy in my work at all anymore were new to him,. I think the totality of my ennui was still a surprise to him. I talked about the death of the young pilot in training exercises with the TA and the next one who died in Capella, and then back to Evelyn's death. I talked about you being missing, declared dead again, and round and round. And I talked about how I didn't want to mourn you because I don't believe or want to believe you're actually dead. He understands how death weighs on the soul from his career in Spaceborne Rescue. He was so empathetic—when he got a little teary-eyed in his memories, he set me off completely. Snot, drool, tears, the whole undignified deal.

I asked him if he believed you are still out there, trying to get home, or if I need to just stop hoping and move on. He said he was sure you are trying to get home, that it's clear how much we love each other, and that he believes you would do whatever it took to not leave me alone. But he also said that we don't know when that might happen, and that I needed to start living life while I could. We talked about money and career, and my complete lack of any civilian skills. He asked me to stay with him and help him out at the restaurant. In a twist of luck for me, he had just lost his host, so your mom's job was open again, though I can do a lot more than that here. I kind of know most of the jobs now. He said he has been thinking of my potential life as a civilian before now, and he has some ideas about jobs that would match my skill set.

He said he knows a veteran who flies locally, and he wants me to meet them. He agreed that I am making the right decision to resign my commission, given my emotional state and the boatload of trauma I am dragging around with me. And the embryo, of course. It was good to hear from someone else that I wasn't just making a snap decision.

I will submit my resignation on Monday. I suddenly feel so free, Andrew, like a set of weights just slipped off my shoulders that I hadn't even realized were there for years. I'm actually smiling. When you come home, you are going to be so shocked. I can't wait to see your face!

Love,
H.

March 23rd, 2122
Joint Base Goose Bay

Andrew,

I did it. I resigned in Colonel Harris' office.

He said he understood completely, and that he was a little surprised I hadn't done this a while ago. He said he is not at all happy to lose me, and he presented a different option—joining the active reserve list. Going Reserve gets me out of a combat billet, lets me live where I want, allows me to keep working toward full retirement, and most important, lets me stay in the immediate versus delayed loop with *Washington* and Lanky developments. All I have to do is maintain my flight readiness, train on new birds when the military puts them into service, and serve in extreme emergencies. Those are the kind of emergencies I would absolutely want to be able to fight, honestly, like a Lanky incursion onto Earth. It really is the best of all worlds. I'll be assigned to Joint Base Burlington for my Reserve home base. The Colonel let me make the transfer immediately because it's only been a month since you were declared deceased and I was due a simple bereavement resignation more than six months ago. He told me that there would always be a door open if I decided I wanted to come back to active duty.

Then I went to my office to finalize the last after action report of my career I'll probably ever write (I wrote most of it while I was on the way here from 51 Pegasi, so I just had to edit it and sign off). Then I sent out a bunch of messages to my colleagues, to let them know of my decision and express my hope to see them before I left in a few days. I'll still have a Fleet PDP, but the address will change from general milnet to the reserve sublist. Then I started packing up my personal stuff in one of those single purpose boxes the Fleet gives out, the same one your stuff came in from Iceland. I've seen other people carry these out of their offices for the last time before, but I never really imagined me doing that before you disappeared.

I'm in our place now, trying to relax. I'm so relieved I can't fully describe it, except that it will definitely help me sleep tonight. I haven't moved your stuff at all since you disappeared. Now, I have move it all, forever. That actually saddens me because these are OUR quarters. That's the second sad thought I've had, the first being leaving my colleagues, sort of friends. I don't have an Evelyn here, so it's only a mild sort of sadness. While I've been typing this note to you, my Fleet PDP has been buzzing like crazy, all my colleagues responding. We're getting together in the OC tomorrow for dinner.

I have one more thing to do tonight other than get chow and go to bed: submit the application to retrieve and carry our embryo. I told you I already started it, all I was missing was an address (which I assumed would be the Chief's place or at least Liberty Falls) and a date of resignation. I had to change that last, as I'm not fully resigned, just changing duty status.

I did it, Andrew. My stomach is fluttering in a combination of girlish excitement and womanly angst. My life has just changed forever, again.

I have really started going gray since you disappeared. Stress will do that to you. I think the gray I have grown will just make me look your age when you get back. You've been going gray with stress for longer than I have. The difference is that it looks really good on you. I love how you look in your last message to me, with those distinguished gray wings in your hair. My gray is not so nice looking, just kind of spread out and most noticeable at my roots. But I don't really mind. Every time I look into the mirror, I'll use it as a reminder that we got old enough to start going gray. So many of the kids from Basic Training Platoon 1066 didn't get that privilege.

Love,
H.

March 27th, 2122
Liberty Falls, VT

Andrew,

Getting off base took me longer than I thought. I had to hand all my open business off to my XO, who will be running the shop until they either give him a new CO or promote him into my old chair.

Wrapping up conversations, investigations, personnel movement, student scores, and more. So much paperwork. All the last last things I did were bittersweet, to my surprise. But final goodbyes are always like that, I guess—except with my mother, that is. All our stuff is in transit to Joint Base Burlington, and will be delivered here tomorrow.

One other last thing I decided to do from my official node was apply for your retirement account to be transferred to our savings account. I felt so predatory. I know I'm the one who suggested we get married for this exact reason when I proposed, but the act of doing it felt like I was taking something from you. I hadn't filed for that fund yet because I didn't need the money, and I didn't want to do anything at all that felt like I was saying goodbye to you. I'm not giving up on you, of course, but I will have to provide at least for myself and hopefully our child someday. My brain has to shift to civilian thinking where people have to spend money just about every day rather than only on those rare leaves from the service. Plus, the Chief told me to do it. He said if the Fleet wants to believe you're dead, them let them do all the things they should for me. And you know what? He's right. We have given so much to the military—our youth, our blood, our sweat, our lives.

I worked my first official day at the restaurant today. It was fun. The customers were all pleasant and smiling. I helped clean the place after we closed, and the work just felt good. No risk of death, no sneaking around monsters. But I'm feeling like a duck out of water during the off hours. It's a liberated feeling, but also a sort of drowning feeling, drowning in silence and idleness. I have never had so much time in which to do nothing (since before I enlisted—and it's hard to remember that far back). When you get back, we are going to talk so much and have <u>that</u> talk in person. I don't think I could ever bear to see you off to battle again.

    Love,
    H.

March 29th, 2122
Liberty Falls, VT

Andrew,

The Chief told me about a job opening. He thinks it would be perfect for me, and I am intrigued enough to consider it. The civilian medical center in Burlington will be looking for a least one pilot for their medevac birds. His friend Barry joined us for dinner tonight. He's a TA and HD veteran, and he is a wealth of helpful information for me. Barry currently flies a Medevac craft for the trauma center, and he'll be retiring from that position soon. He came to meet me and talk about the job tonight. And I think the Chief may be right.

Barry told me that the job is mostly being on stand-by, like any ambulance, ready to leave at any time during my shift, but only during my shift. There is revolving on-call time, too, when a pilot has to report to work off-schedule due to an accident, but time on duty is significantly less than in the Fleet. We talked about other jobs he held after he retired from the military, one of which was flying commercial airlines. That was the first job that occurred to me when I thought of retiring. We talked at length about it, and why he left it to fly locally. He said flying commercially has different, but as many stresses as the military, and it's a huge time commitment flying back and forth on the same routes. He said he got bored with it very quickly. And lots of other drawbacks like having to deal with the paying and sometimes unhappy and rowdy public. So that's not for me. You know I'm not the kind of person to take lip from some blowhard civilian over a wrong seat assignment or some nonsense like that.

I am feeling so much lighter without all the stresses of Fleet bullshit, and I really don't want to replace them with new ones. At the end of Barry's visit, I decided I would apply for the position he is leaving. He told me to move quickly, so that's my first move tomorrow after a good night's sleep.

I received my first official communication from the Defense District Command, and I'm to report to Joint Base Burlington on Monday for indoctrination to Reserve status, expectations, and duties. I'm sure it'll be a blast.

Love,
H.

April 1st, 2122
Liberty Falls, VT

Andrew,

    I finally got an official letter from the Reproductive Board. They slotted me in for an interview on June 12th. At first I was irritated that it was so far off. Now that I'm ready to do this, I'm ready to do this. You know me. But I made myself calm down by reading may homework. It turns out I have a lot to do between now and then, and I'll need to reschedule if I haven't completed all my tasks before then. I need to get blood tests to test for pregnancy hormones at specific points in my cycle and fill out charts on my own to know when I'm at those points.

    The Reproductive Board will do the initial blood-testing and implant the fertilized egg when my body is ready, but they don't provide the OB care during gestation or delivery, so I have to establish care with an OB-GYN in Burlington, probably at the hospital where I want to apply. The job isn't listed yet, so I can't apply yet.

    In the meantime, the literature says that my body should recover pretty quickly from the birth control cocktail the military keeps us on while we're in combat billets, especially at my age. But I have to keep track of my cycles now. And I'll need to get supplies I haven't thought about in years. That far off date in June is so my body can get back to its normal cycle that has been totally disrupted for over a decade and I have recored at least two cycles. That makes sense. We're on the way, Andrew.

Love,
H.

April 5th, 2122
Liberty Falls, VT

Andrew,

This has never excited me before, but I needed those supplies today. It's only been two weeks, but my body was clearly ready to get back to normal. I'll spare you the details, but the Reproductive Board info indicated that this could happen quickly, depending on age and health, so it looks like I'm in probably in good health and my body still thinks it's young. The next step is finding an OB-GYN.

The restaurant was very busy today. The whole town was packed with people getting outside now that mud season is almost over. I went for a run after we closed and cleaned up. The ornamental cherry trees are starting to bloom. It's beautiful out there. You'll be here to enjoy this next year.

Love,
H.

April 6th, 2122
Liberty Falls, VT

Andrew,

I reported to Joint Base Burlington this morning for INDOC into the Reserves. It was pretty anticlimactic, just paperwork and informational stuff. I get to keep my flight status current, and I have to take part in readiness exercises once a year. Oh, and I got to hang on to a bunch of my issued gear, like the helmet and the flight suits. I don't have an assigned reserve unit—the idea is that I'll get assigned where I'm needed if the balloon goes up and I get called in for emergencies.

During INDOC, I was one of only three officers in the room, and the other two were both lieutenants. I don't think they get too many O-5s in the Reserves because I had to stop the sergeant on duty from calling the room to attention when I walked in.

At first I was a little conflicted about keeping the uniform and giving them a rope on which to pull me back in, but now I think it was the right decision. It keeps me on MilNet and in the loop, and I'll have something to do other than just duck and hope for the best if the Lankies ever make it back to Earth again.

Love,
H.

April 15th, 2122
Liberty Falls, VT

Andrew,

Life is really busy right now, but in a really good and distracting way. I applied for that medevac job at the Burlington trauma center as soon as it showed up as available on the hospital's net node, which was this morning. Now I am just waiting and hoping for a call to interview. In the meantime, I looked up a few other jobs that are open to pilots. One of them is for a photography and touring company, flying tourists around the Green Mountains. I haven't applied for that one because it sounds pretty boring to me. The medevac position seems more like professional home, like flying SAR birds, essentially.

This makes me think of you, of course, but almost everything does, either by association or because I want to talk to you about it. I wonder what kind of job you might get on Earth—aside from the Lazarus Brigades. Now that I'm settling into civilian life and have lost all the pressures of being responsible for the lives of all those young pilots, I don't think I could handle going back into a war-like zone in the PRCs, or be happy with you going there. I'll keep thinking about possibilities for you, though. There are so many jobs available for civilians that might work for ex-Fleet. Just think of my dad—he's military R&D, but he doesn't have an ounce of real military experience. You would be so much better at that than him. You'd have to earn your degree in Engineering. Just a thought.

I've been doing civilian things anytime I'm not helping the Chief. I had to go clothes shopping, but had no idea where to go or what to buy, so the Chief directed me to a little store in Liberty Falls to a person who helped me find a few starter sets. So far, I've been walking to my destinations because Liberty Falls is so condensed and the Chief's Place is so central, and I've taken the maglev to Burlington a couple of times, but eventually I'm going to have to get a license and a small vehicle. So I picked up a study guide to learn the rules of the roads, and the Chief is teaching me to drive his car on Tuesdays and Wednesdays, the days he doesn't open his restaurant. We eat at other restaurants while we're out and that's fun to compare the menu, decor, and service to the Chief's place.

Once again, I think the shrink was on target to have me write these letters to you, despite my initial reluctance. It seemed a little like pretentious navel-gazing at first, but now I don't think I could do without it. I'm still seeing the shrink via vidcall monthly, and he has commented on how positive the changes I've made seem to be on my mental health. So, I keep going with it. And I can't wait for you to read it.

Love,
H.

April 17th, 2122

Andrew,

I got my first blood draw at the RB office today. I'm midway through my first full cycle. I don't get any results for now, they're just compiling data.

Love,
H.

April 30th, 2122
Liberty Falls, VT

Andrew,

    I think of you all the time, every day, but I find that I'm mostly content to wait for you at the moment because I'm really busy making a life for us here, and my daily life is becoming somewhat routine for me.

    Today, something out of the ordinary happened: I had a civilian job interview! My interviewer was a woman named Jillian, and she is in charge of the three medevac ships and six pilots in the group. She has never been in the military, so my background stories left her gaping sometimes, particularly whenever I mentioned the Lankies. She continued to ask questions unrelated to the Medevac job. She even thanked me for my service and might have shown a bit of hero worship—at least genuine awe. I'm not sure because that's never been directed at me before. It was weird and a little uncomfortable. Those things were just part of the job, and no one was considered a hero except maybe the Medal of Honor recipients.

    So, I deflected to you. I told her about your job because it's more dangerous than mine, and because some of your bare escapes are so by-the-hair-of-your-teeth that they do inspire awe, like the drop ship you were in that got skewered by a penetrator. I was really enjoying the talk and the memories and I had a willing audience. It was strange to me because I've never thought about how extraordinary and completely beyond the understanding of most people on Earth our jobs are. You know everyone hates a braggart in the Corps. But she had no idea about my job performance, so I had to share it, which did make me feel like a braggart at the end. But I could tell she didn't see it that way at all, especially when I told her about being in the Battle for Earth in Detroit. She'd heard about it, saw it on the news, and I think it just increased her awe. If the goal of an interview is to made a good first impression, like the Chief advised, I think I nailed it. Jillian wants more details, more answers about Lankies, which is a thing I can give her. So if I wasn't already fully qualified to fly (after orientation to these birds, of course), I'd have another in.

I asked if my intent to get pregnant would be a problem. She said that by law, it can't be a problem, and that it would not influence her decision to hire me if I was the right applicant. She told me there was one other applicant she still had to interview for the one open pilot slot. She will let me know in about a week.

I shared this information with the Chief, and he thinks I have a really good shot at the position. I helped him in the restaurant for the dinner shift, and we talked as usual while cleaning up after we closed. He told me he would list a job opening and start interviewing my replacement because he just had a strong feeling that I would get an offer. I insisted on paying him fair rent if it worked out rather than continuing to stay here for trade. He agreed to let me, but we haven't discussed how much yet. If I get the job, it definitely won't be a problem. We owe him so much for everything he's done for both of us and your mom. It will make me feel better to begin paying him. Making up for all the past kindnesses will be another struggle and will take time. I'm confident I'll have that time now.

Love,
H.

May 6th, 2122
Liberty Falls, VT

Andrew,

I got the job! I will soon be flying as a civilian medevac pilot for the trauma hospital in Burlington. I really like that. It comes with great perks, too, or so the Chief says. I'm still trying to figure out how things work, so he had to explain the benefits to me—six weeks annual vacation time. That's double what the military gives us, and it's apparently better than average for civilian jobs, too. I get a retirement account they contribute to along with me, so it grows faster than the military retirement. There's maternity health insurance, and more perks that I haven't figured out yet, I'm sure. The Joint Base Burlington hospital doesn't do maternity, so I need that additional insurance according to the Chief, who is much more savvy with the civvie life stuff than I am. He says the salary is great, so I'll have no trouble paying rent, and he doesn't mind accepting it. I'll be able to buy the little car I will need to commute instead of taking the maglev and having to walk from and to the stations. And I'll be able to add to our savings to buy a house for us. I'm feeling really good right now, Andrew.

Life is in motion and all the new things I'm experiencing, learning, and living are excellent for keeping my worries in check. I am so excited for you to join me here.

Love,
H.

May 11th, 2122
Burlington, VT

Andrew,

 Today was my first and only day of INDOC, or "orientation" in civilian-speak, for my new pilot job.
 It was so much less pomp and circumstance than the military. It had none, in fact, except some silly games and a swag bag of hospital-labeled paraphernalia like a water bottle, pens, a notebook, and a T-shirt. I also got several collared shirts and a jacket that are my official uniform, basically. It was conducted by an HR person and it involved getting a badge, work node address, and company PDP; sitting through lectures about corporate policies, goals and mission statements; and meeting all the other new hires through a sitting-circle sharing process that felt like grade school. I was the only ex-military person there as far as anyone shared. They were mostly nurses, a few doctors, a pharmacy tech, and support staff. The only other person I will run into again was a man roughly my age, John Mason, who is a medevac and ground ambulance EMT. He has done that job for about 10 years at another hospital in another state, and moved to VT for this job. I'll be seeing him when we're on the same shift. Then I went on a tour of the hospital with the entire group. The tour was pretty superficial because of patient privacy. Patient privacy was a class all by itself in which we learned how to very specifically protect patient information. I'm so used to keeping details classified that this really seemed like the easiest thing to learn—old hat, really. Civilians are afforded a lot more privacy than we are in the military by law, so part of my job is not revealing people's health situations by name or any other identifying factors. That's pretty easy.
 Another part of the orientation was filling out tons of paperwork. Paperwork for getting paid into our VT bank account the Chief took me to set up, for setting up another retirement account, for paying taxes, for getting partial healthcare insurance. (We don't need full coverage because we can go to the med center at Joint Base Burlington for just about everything, but if all goes well in a few months, I'll be using the maternity ward here in the future and will find my maternity doc here.

The end of my tour was one-on-one with John. We went to the landing pads on top of the hospital and oriented to the elevators, hallways, and entrance to the trauma center and ER. Though my job really begins and ends on the landing pad, I'm expected to help transport in a pinch. All in all, it was a totally relaxed day compared to the military dog-and-pony shows. I liked it, Andrew.

My primary job will be flying, maintaining the craft mechanically, and communicating with flight control. However, I'll be expected to help with patients if necessary, so I need to be able to do basic emergency medical intervention. Barry retires in two weeks, and Jillian wants me on the job as soon as I can get my type familiarization done. She told me that Barry recommended me for the position, and his opinion apparently carries a lot of weight with her. It's nice to be thought of so well by people I've barely met.

Love,
H.

May 15th, 2122
Liberty Falls, VT

Andrew,

I established care with an OB-GYN today. Her name is Dr. McCauley Lowell and she is about ten years younger than I am. She's familiar with IVF, of course, and she knows about the Reproductive Board. She also did a pelvic exam and told me that I am actually ovulating right now (!), which is a little off a perfectly normal cycle. She told me to get to the RB office today to get another blood test. In all, it was good news and I'm hopeful all will be well with our bundle of cells.

In other news—not quite as exciting, but important—I agreed to meet my father early in Boston next weekend. I will stay the evening and head back on Sunday. We are going to a classical music performance and dinner and having breakfast and lunch Sunday before we both go back to our different homes. It will be a really quick visit, but at least I'm giving him the time. He seems grateful and eager. I wish I was as excited as he is. I asked him not to tell my mother when we worked out the place, dates, and times and he promised me he didn't. He still doesn't know *Washington* is missing. I'm not sure I'm going to tell him about that, or the possible pregnancy. I will see whether I trust him enough to share some of my worries and hopes.

Love,
H.

May 18th, 2122
Liberty Falls, VT

Andrew,

I started my type familiarization on the medevac craft today. The hospital's flight department uses the Textron AV-21. It's atmospheric flight only, of course, and a whole different beast than a military drop ship. It's less than half the size—I swear it could probably fit into the back of a Wasp—but it's much more nimble and responsive. My old Dragonfly feels like a tugboat by comparison.

I'll be doing the familiarization for the next two days, and then I'll be cleared for flying in the left seat as co-pilot. The requirement for Pilot-in-command status is two hundred hours, which they said should only take me a few months at their operational pace.

Imagine—I'm back in the apprentice seat even though I have thousands of flight hours on military drop ships. But those are the rules, and none of the pretty ribbons the Corps gave me can buy any shortcuts in this world.

Love,
H.

May 22nd, 2122
Liberty Falls, VT

Andrew,

I am feeling pretty good. I gave the Chief my first rent check and he actually accepted it. His gratitude makes me feel guilty for all the years we didn't pay him, but he's having none of it. He gave me a little lecture on how important we are to him, that we've become the family he never could have, that we have kept him in the military loop, and so on. Then he said I might allow him to be a grandfather, which is a thing he had never even dreamed of. He kept going until I admitted he was right.

His excitement over the possible pregnancy makes me worry a little, which is exactly the wrong feeling to be having according to the handouts from the OB's office. Stress makes pregnancies fail.

I'm done with the type familiarization on the AV-21. Next week, I'll start flying on calls in the left seat with one of the senior pilots.

I take the maglev to Boston tomorrow to spend some time with Dad. I have very mixed feelings about this, but at least I won't have to tolerate it long if I don't like it.

Love,
H.

May 24th, 2122
Liberty Falls, VT

Andrew,

    I took the maglev to Boston and met Dad at our hotel yesterday. On the way in, I saw the PRC clusters. I don't know which one you grew up in, and it doesn't matter, but the sight filled my mind with thoughts of you and your mother, which made me furious with my mother all over again when I recall how she disrespected you in her home. I had to rein in my temper so I didn't meet Dad in anger. It wasn't easy, let me tell you.
    The visit with him went well. He is still his old self, but he has visibly aged a lot—like we all have, I suppose. It <u>has</u> been eight years. He hugged me tightly when he saw me, and there were tears in his eyes when I pulled back. We went to a Vivaldi Four Seasons performance, like we used to do when I still lived at home before I enlisted. I loved it; it soothed me in a way only good memories can. I didn't have to suppress my anger at all.
    Dinner was an expensive seafood affair with a whole lobster each, pilaf, steamed vegetables, mashed potatoes, and a lot more. Dessert and wine, too. The military chow has never been so good as that. It was a lot of food and the meal was long, so we had a lot of time to talk. At the end I felt guilty for depriving him of his only child all these years. Now that I am approaching the chance to be a mother, I thought about how I would feel in his place, and it amped up my guilt. He's always been ruled by my mother, but he was always the better, more loving parent. He paid for the hotel and the meals, even though I tried to beat him to the tab. But he said he really, really, really wanted to do this for me, so I relented.
    I did not tell him about the embryo. I did, however, tell him about *Washington,* and he expressed what I felt was genuine worry for you. He said he knows how much I love you, if only from the performance I gave at his house the last time we saw him and my mother, and especially the fact that I am not over my anger at her. I told him that if anything my anger is more intense under the circumstances. I learned things about him and his relationship with my mother I only sort of knew, such as the fact that she's abusive to him both verbally and emotionally. I asked why he never left her, and he said

it was because of me, and that now as he's nearing retirement, he realizes he doesn't want to spend his downtime with her. I asked him if he is going to divorce her now that I'm not in the picture, and he told me that he has already been speaking with a lawyer.

    I decided that I will spend time with him again. I think he needs it. Maybe I do, too. I'll talk to the Chief about it.

    Love,
    H.

May 26th, 2122
Liberty Falls, VT

Andrew,

We never really celebrated holidays in the military. We never knew where we were going to be, so there were no scheduled holidays other than the few select religious ones. In civilian life, we definitely take holidays. Yesterday was a holiday, Memorial Day, carried over from the old USA, meant to commemorate military war veterans who died in the service. I got the day off, so I helped the Chief out. Holidays are good business for restaurants because civvies are out spending money on their holiday, and they always need food sooner or later. He hired a host, so I worked as his sous chef, chopping everything he needed, peeling and crushing garlic, grating ginger, squeezing lemons, making sauces, and more.

The significance of the holiday was not lost on me. You were on my mind all day long. But you're not dead, Andrew! You're likely not even lost. You know exactly where you are. Just because I don't doesn't mean you're not on your way back to me. I haven't thought about Masoud in a long time, but sometimes I still wonder if he might be behind this. God help him if I ever find out that he is.

Love,
H

May 28th, 2122
Liberty Falls, VT

Andrew,

Today I sat in the left seat in the hospital craft while we did a patient pick-up. I thought my days in the left seat were long over, so this was a little surreal. The pilot is James Leach, and he's been in this job for 14 years. He is a fabulous PIC. He's calm and laid back, and that helped me rein in my split interpretation of action. My brain is ingesting new terms. This is not an SAR bird, it's a Medevac bird, although in my mind, they are the same. I'll have so much less to do as a pilot in this situation. There will be no Lankies to kill while making a rescue, no terrible atmospheres to beat up the ship on the way to the deck. It feels too easy. I'm sure there's more to it than I'm imagining.

Love,
H.

June 5th, 2122
Liberty Falls, VT

Andrew,

Today, I saw some of the dangerous sides of being a medevac pilot.

James and I had to pick up patients on a roadway in the middle of a messy multi-car accident scene. No Lankies, but it was pretty tense. James had to land quite precisely among vehicles that were crumpled, some of which were smoking like they were ready to go up. The fire department came roaring in and firemen spilled out of the truck and swarmed the scene. The ground ambulances and police were already there, and they directed us to our landing spot. One of our EMTs leaped out when we were settling on the ground with barely a word to us and ran to the car the firefighters were coating with fire retardant. He was back by the time we fully landed, grabbing gear, a gurney, and his co-EMT. They rushed to the nearest vehicle that was upside down. The firefighters were prying open the door when they got there. Once they got the patient out of the car, they had to triage on the ground. She was losing blood and clearly in a lot pain, still conscious. Once they had her on a gurney, they hauled her back to the craft, and we took off in a hurry while they were still hooking up her IV.

It may sound weird, but it sort of felt like home, like a military medevac on the battlefield, except the patient was wearing a green pant suit instead of battle armor. But this call confirmed in my mind that I'm in the right place.

Love,
H.

June 12th, 2122
Liberty Falls, VT

Andrew,

    I had my interview with the Maternity Board at 1300. I thought it would be confrontational, that I'd have to brow-beat them into letting me carry our embryo to term, but it was exactly the opposite.

    I brought my tracking chart for my cycle. I'm a little irregular, which they say sometimes correlates with hormone imbalance and is really common. Their blood tests did not reveal any specific abnormalities, and both the tracking and the testing put me firmly in the ideal range for IVF procedure parameters. I learned something right away that both of us missed—we have four fertilized eggs, not just one. I must have been too angry with my mother at the time for that to register, but I don't know how you missed it. (Hah.)

    This Board is a service provided to the military that is free of charge to active duty or retired personnel, so we're in good shape. I always assumed IVF would not cost much, but it turns out that it is astoundingly expensive and would not be covered by my insurance with the hospital at all because I am still fertile and have no history of difficulty getting pregnant. Without you here, there will be no history of difficulty getting pregnant, so hurrah for the Maternity Board. Ultimately, it is a perk for those of us who risk it all while in service, so I'm happier with this whole set-up now that I have a broader understanding. There is no approval needed—just my tests, the tracking chart for best timing, and an appointment when the best time is established.

    The OB-GYN, Captain Choi, performed a pelvic exam using this clamp thing that literally exposed everything inside me. Dr. Choi saw what's good news for us: the lucky fact is that I'm ovulating again today, and that is exactly when implantation should happen. And they had the time and the room because I was the only patient there, so they actually did the implantation procedure today.

    They implanted one of our four embryos! Today has just been a whirlwind of new info and procedures. Now we wait. I'll take a home pregnancy test in a week. These embryos grew 5 days before they were frozen, so they're mature enough to show up on a test five to seven days post-implantation.

    Andrew, I am so damned excited—I don't know when you'll be home in this process, but no matter when, I know that you are going to be as rocked to your core as I was when *Washington* disappeared. I absolutely cannot wait to see it!

    All my love,
    H.

June 14th, 2122
Liberty Falls, VT

Andrew,

    I went on another harrowing medevac run today. According to James, it wasn't particularly unusual, so I am getting a bit of perspective regarding the amounts of blood civilian medevac pilots get to see compared to their military counterparts. Let's just say that even with all the automated transportation, the laws of physics still exist, and high-speed collisions between cars can cause injuries that are every bit as messy and gruesome as battlefield wounds from artillery or gunfire. More, really, because civvies aren't wearing any armor.
    Maybe I should hold off on that license and keep taking the maglev for a while...

Love,
H.

June 20th, 2122
Liberty Falls, VT

Andrew,

It's a weird thing to be able to type out, but here goes: I am pregnant with our baby!

It hasn't been a week yet. I left a message with the Maternity Board because they told me to contact them as soon as I had a positive test, but today is Saturday, so I won't hear back from them until Monday. I also left a message with Dr. Lowell, but nobody's there either and I won't hear back until Monday because it's not an emergency despite what my adrenaline is telling me.

I told the Chief and he is in no better state of mind than I am, which is to say, a bouncy, excited, unable to stop mass of cells. We barely managed to pull off dinner at the restaurant tonight. Andrew, I feel fabulous. I wish you could feel this, but I know you're struggling to get home. If you could feel what I feel, you would have so much hope. I'll feel it for you. Be safe.

Love,
H.

June 22nd, 2122
Liberty Falls, VT

Andrew,

    I just had an appointment with the Maternity Board. I still think that's a really odd name for a bunch of OB-GYN docs and nurses. It's not a Board so much as a cryovault inside a doctor's office that's fully staffed. I'm just calling it the MB from now on. I don't know why they don't follow their patients to the birth, but they don't—they hand us off after the first trimester. It must be one of those old, stupid rules that nobody has bothered to update in the modern era. But that's what I'm stuck with, so I'll just have to deal with it.

    Now that I've had any first appointment and implantation, they got me in right away. Today, they used ultrasound to look at at my womb and the embryo that has taken residence. It's hard to describe the visual chaos that is an ultrasound if you have not had one explained to you, but I could see a clear outline of what they call an egg sac and the embryo nestled into a wall of that sac. So there's visual confirmation of this pregnancy. I won't know anything else about the embryo for quite a while. It has a lot of work to do dividing itself and organizing those new cells. It's a pretty astounding process when you learn about it. Science again, pulling me in its direction. I feel elated and bouncy mentally, but nothing physically yet. The doc tells me that is exactly as it should be. So far, so good. My next appointment is on July 22nd.

Love,
H.

June 29th, 2122
Liberty Falls, VT

Andrew,

This past week, I've been in basic EMT training, which takes place primarily in the classroom, but a little on the job as well. We performed a couple of transports from rural hospitals and once, from an isolated cabin in the woods to the trauma center. I'm continuing to pile up hours in the bird and hours with patients, so all of my training is going well and fast. Everything seems to be going well with the pregnancy, too. I'm feeling the elation I read about that comes with the pregnancy hormones flooding my system. All is well. I hope you are warm (or cool, whatever makes you more comfortable wherever you are right now), safe, and on your way back to me.

Love,
H.

July 6th, 2122
Liberty Falls, VT

Andrew,

Work, training, and the pregnancy continue. Nothing new there, but the Chief and I have been talking about real estate. I've been telling him that it's not practical to keep a baby in his restaurant. He argued at first, but he came to see my point eventually. So we've started collecting real estate listings on the net. I want something as close to the Chief as I can get and he wants that, too. The fetus is totally quiet, though I know it's busy dividing, dividing, and dividing, somehow becoming something amazing.

Love,
H.

July 11th, 2122
Liberty Falls, VT

Andrew,

I have very bad news. All my elation from the past week is dried up, but ready to come right back. This morning, I started having menstrual cramps, so I called the FB and they saw me right away. The Chief drove me and was with me for the heartbreak, holding my hand. The egg sac was collapsing visibly on the ultrasound and it can't be saved, so I miscarried. The crushing feeling I felt just then was like hearing *Washington* was missing again. If we had seen it as it just started to happen, they think they could have stopped it. They said that miscarriages are totally normal and happen very often, especially as a woman gets older. In my case, what they discovered is that I have a luteal phase defect. Sounds harsh, but they assured me that me that it is very easily fixed.

Here's what happened: my body stops making progesterone too soon or doesn't produce enough progesterone continuously, and the progesterone is what makes and maintains the egg sac. That's why my cycle is irregular. But, the problem is easily fixed by taking oral progesterone while I'm pregnant.

We have a new plan. We are waiting a few months after the D&C to let my body recover and fully prepare itself again, so I continue tracking. We are aiming for a September retry.

I am incredibly disappointed and so is the Chief, but the MB seems very confident in their assessment and plan. Their confidence is consoling to us both, so we just keep going forward now.

Love,
H.

July 18th, 2122
Liberty Falls, VT

Andrew,

I'm just checking to tell you I'm doing fine and looking forward to my next appointment with the FB on the 31st.

I keep racking up flight hours and EMT hours in class and on the job. I am a genuine grease monkey now. I can service the whole bird. I knew how to do emergency service on the Blackflies and Dragonflies, but I never did regular maintenance. I don't love it, but it's part of the job. Turns out it's actually kind of satisfying to get your hands dirty every now and then.

Love,
H.

July 25th, 2122
Liberty Falls, VT

Andrew,

I went to my first readiness exercise in the Reserves. It involved me going up to Joint Base Burlington and spending a day at the firing range with some new Corps hardware, then another two days at the airfield getting reacquainted with the controls of a drop ship and doing some practice circuits around the lake. With the new job, I'm not lacking any cockpit time lately, but it was still fun to fly one of the military ships again, even if it was a clapped-out TA Wasp and not my old Dragonfly. Turns out the atmospheric junkers can still go five hundred knots at two hundred feet above the lake. Or so I've heard.

Love,
H.

July 31st, 2122
Liberty Falls, VT

Andrew,

I went to the FB today, and they looked at my womb. I'm building a normal egg sac, "happily getting ready for an egg" according to them. So far, so good.

Love,
H

August 10th, 2122
Liberty Falls, VT

Andrew,

Happy Anniversary! 10 years, my love. I want more years, and I want you to here to share those years. I hope you're almost home. I know that when it happens, it will be all of a sudden for me. You'll just appear one day and no one will see it coming. It will be so different from your perspective, I know. I miss you.

All is well this week. Work continues exactly as before, more hours under my belt. The Chief and I started looking at houses. We found a great piece of property in Liberty Falls just a block from the Chief's Place, but there's no house on it yet. I've never thought of building a house, but the idea is really exciting now that the Chief suggested it.

I watched your last message to me and your suit telemetry. I can't tell you how much comfort those two things give me.

Love,
H.

August 20th, 2122
Liberty Falls, VT

Andrew,

I had an appointment at the FB today. I'm ovulating again and the lining looks great, but they want to wait until my next cycle to try again. Again, they are confident and that reassures me. In three weeks, they want me to come every day to monitor me more closely. Today, there was actually another patient there. Her name is Amelia, and she's a nurse at the Veteran's hospital on the Base. She's former Territorial Army, Med Corps, and about 10 years older than me. She stayed in until full retirement. She's originally from Ottawa, which I found a little ironic. It made me like her by association, but as we talked I came to like her in truth.

Her process will be a lot more complicated than mine because she's older. And, like me, she's alone in this process. I will definitely be seeing her again and I'm looking forward to it.

Love,
H.

August 29th, 2122
Liberty Falls, VT

Andrew,

I'm exhausted from a few long days in a row of transport flights all over the Northeast. New York was the worst because the city sky is so crowded down there—you spend more time talking to ATC and listening to their directions than anything else. I find I don't like looking at so much urban space after being in the Green Mountains for so long.

In reproductive news, everything is perfect, a womb-in-waiting. Next week, I'll be going to the FB every day.

Love,
H.

September 10th, 2122
Liberty Falls, VT

Andrew,

I finally passed my required flight hours to qualify for pilot-in-command status, and Jillian wasted no time assigning me as shift lead. We have two new pilots coming in to take the load off the existing ones a bit, and I'm getting one of them as co-pilot.

I thought I was in the cockpit a lot when I was still a junior officer in the Corps, but it's pretty amazing how much more flying the medevac teams get in. There isn't a shift that goes by where I am not in the air at some point. And every minute of it is spent with a good purpose. In the Corps, most of my stick time was training and exercise. Here, I have a vital mission every single time I lift off, trying to save lives. It feels satisfying in a way I can't really describe, even when it's stressful. I know that a lot of people only lived because we were there to fly them to the trauma center at top speed. It makes me feel like I'm clawing back some of the lives from the universe that I've lost in my command over the years.

Love,
H.

September 12th, 2122
Liberty Falls, VT

Andrew,

We own a house lot in Liberty Falls!

I'm not sure what I'll do with it yet, and part of me is resistant to the idea of starting anything before you're back with me. This will be your home as well, after all. It seems wrong to not get your input. But we need a place to call our own before our child is born because I don't want to raise it in a little apartment above a busy restaurant. If you really hate it, we can always tear it down and build it again, right?

The options are overwhelming, though, and I don't know enough about this stuff to make an educated decision yet. There's modular, 3D-printed, all-timber, brick, prefab concrete...sometimes I am so overloaded by choice that I just want to drive around until I see a house I like and tell them to copy that. But then it wouldn't be just ours, would it?

Love,
H.

Sept. 18th, 2122
Liberty Falls, VT

Andrew,

Today the FB implanted the second embryo. Today was day 2 after I started ovulating, and the lining looks perfect. They gave me a bottle of oral progesterone to start, and I'll be back every other day after a positive pregnancy test except the weekends unless there's an emergency. Amelia was there as well, and so was another woman and her partner. That's busiest I've ever seen it. I invited Amelia to come to the Chief's Place for great food and maybe more. They have a lot in common.

Love,
H.

September 25th, 2122
Liberty Falls, VT

Andrew,

We are pregnant again! I got a positive test today and I went to the FB, where they visually confirmed it and did a blood test. I'm so full of needle holes, I look like I'm sick or an addict. My progesterone is in the normal range, so all is well.

Love,
H.

October 2nd, 2122
Liberty Falls, VT

Andrew,

It's fall in the Green Mountains, and it is glorious. I feel fantastic. I know it's pregnancy hormones because Jennifer Barns, my new doula, tells me so and I read it in a pregnancy book, too. But you aren't here for the second year in a row to enjoy this with me. I'm incredibly unhappy—not grieving, but despairing when I think of you and how long you've been gone. The pregnancy hormones pull me up out of the despair, then I think of the fact that you should be here, and my mood goes down again, then back up. It's a really disconcerting ride. Gods, I miss you.

But—I have another week of positive news. The pregnancy continues normally, the fetus is growing, I feel great again, the Chief is happy, but he has started treating me like an invalid. We have been talking to contractors and doulas. The doula was his idea and he lined up a couple of interviews for me. They're like pregnancy coaches and he is paying for this himself. He says because he wants all the answers, but I think it's because he wants a bigger role in this whole journey. We decided on Jennifer. She actually reminds me of Evelyn a little, both in her mannerisms and because she loves to quote scientific studies. The Chief is reassured by her apparent knowledge.

Getting to fly for the trauma center in the fall is a major job perk all by itself. If you think a New England fall looks amazing from ground level, you should see it from the air—a carpet of red and orange, green and yellow as far as the eye can see. One day I'll be able to take you up so you can look at it yourself.

Love,
H.

October 9th, 2122
Liberty Falls, VT

Andrew,

 I went for a run today and stopped for a long time at your mother's grave to cry and laugh with her for a bit.
 I wish so badly I could share this with her in life. I can just imagine her fussing over me. I wear her rosary beads all the time now, like a uniform or a shield from the sad thoughts.
 Physically, everything is perfectly fine with me and our fetus. Growth is normal, but it hasn't reached the looks-human stage yet. All of the ultrasounds they've taken are recorded and they will compile a slide show, almost a movie of growth, so you won't miss any of that. The Chief bought me a baby book to record my thoughts feelings, ideas, and so on during the pregnancy. It's another journal, this time for both you and our child. And Jennifer gave me homework. So I'm relaxing in our apartment, reading a book on gestation. I have another on sleep cycles in babies, kids, teens, and adults. I wanted to do science and all this biology has just fallen in my lap.
 One thing I'm learning that is no priority in the military is to destress. Stress is bad on the body and bad for pregnancies. The main stressor in my life is your absence, unfortunately, and there is zero I can do about that except to stay positive. It's so hard to do that, but I swear as soon as I think about our baby (that's part of you in there!), it almost makes me better. Hormones.

Please be safe.

Love,
H.

October 17th, 2122
Liberty Falls, VT

Andrew,

The Chief and I settled on a contractor to build our house today. I still haven't gotten your retirement fund because the Corps hasn't released it yet. I'm going back and forth with them, but it's out of my control and "there's an internal process and extended waiting period" for Missing/Presumed Dead personnel. Luckily, we pooled all of our regular income in a joint account for years, and neither of us touched it, so it's sizable. Now I've got my trauma center income. Also, I took my sign-on bonus as a cash-out, so that's added to the pool. They're still withholding your bonus in addition to your retirement. And I have to say, it makes me feel good, actually. It makes me believe they still think you are going to show up.

That fucking Masoud. If you really are on a clandestine mission, I've never seen tighter mission OPSEC. But again, they're withholding your bonus and retirement for some reason. They released my bonus to me, but my retirement is still building because I went Reserve. My brain keeps going in circles about this, but it keeps my hope alive.

Anyway, I will take out a loan for the construction instead of spending all our money. That's the point of that loopy message. Pregnancy makes me feel good, but it also screws with my memory, reasoning, and logic circuits. I wish you could feel it! Physically, I've been feeling weird neural impulses in my womb area—deep inside, not in the skin. It's gentle, really, just a difference in how my tissue feels below my stomach, behind the lower abdominal muscles. I've never felt it before, but have been since a few weeks after the pregnancy was positive. It's not pain, it's not pleasure, just different sensations. My body knows something is different.

Love,
H.

October 24th 2122
Liberty Falls, VT

Andrew,

The contractors have broken ground on the house site. Our pregnancy is normal, but I am tired and exhausted a lot these days.

The woman I met at the FB, Amelia, came to the Chief's place today. It was a nice visit and felt great to have a leisurely talk with another vet. The Chief sat down and talked for a while, too. And—he invited her back!

Love,
H.

October 31st, 2122
Liberty Falls, VT

Andrew,

It snowed today and everything is beautiful, white, and cold. I had a flashback to New Svalbard when I stepped outside, but it isn't cold enough to maintain the charade for my brain. The contractors have poured the foundation for the house, and the concrete is setting. Now they are pausing work until winter is over.

I am on call this weekend, and I had an emergency flight this morning. Another hiking incident. This time, the hikers thought they were experienced enough to judge the weather. They weren't. It was an easy extraction, though, and they're off the mountain, recovering.

Jennifer went with me to my appointment at the FB yesterday. They said everything looks perfect—my vitals and hormones are all normal.

Love,
H.

November 7th, 2122
Liberty Falls, VT

Andrew,

Yesterday, my military PDP lit up with a slew of message alerts, and I nearly jumped out of my skin. I'm not used to that so much any more, and my thoughts instantly jumped to hopes you had returned. Instead, it was some all-hands update about a Fleet action out of system. A pair of Avengers ran into four seed ships out in Iota Persei and splashed them all without any friendly casualties. Good news, I suppose, but not the kind of good news I've been waiting for.

It'll come, sooner or later. I'm certain of it.

Love,
H.

November 18th, 2122
Liberty Falls, VT

Andrew,

Today is my 36th birthday. I have such mixed feelings today. I am happy, content, hopeful, excited, empty, and in despair in no particular order. I have a baby bump, a healthy pregnancy, a really good job, a loving father-figure in the Chief, a pending home. I have love in my life and I am missing the love of my life. See what I mean?

The Chief made me a cake and lamb stew tonight. I don't know what I would have done without him since you disappeared, Andrew. He has been my anchor. Amelia stopped by to celebrate, too. She brought me a stuffed animal for the baby and a maternity tunic for me. We all watched your suit telemetry so you could be present, too. Amelia was in turn amazed, shocked, horrified, and impressed, as you can imagine. She and the chief got into a deep discussion about their own experiences. There were a lot of smiles exchanged between them. It was a warm and lovely evening. My father sent me birthday greetings, too, and I felt a little guilty because I'm still keeping him at a distance, and he's alone.

I love you.
H.

January 1st, 2123
Liberty Falls, VT

Andrew,

Other than the pregnancy progressing normally, nothing noteworthy has been happening until today. Except that this is the second year now since you've been gone. I have no doubt that you're on one hell of a mission, but I've exhausted my imagination trying to guess what it could be.

I haven't updated this journal for a while because I've been putting all the baby stuff into the baby book the Chief gave me, and you'll be able to read it all there. I don't want to write it out twice. Another holiday season has just passed, but those weren't a big part of our lives before, so this time isn't especially poignant for us as a couple. What is poignant is this part of you I'm carry inside me.

There was one incident that scared me: the Chief is healthy and as active as ever, but he slipped on ice on the sidewalk and fell hard. He didn't break anything, but he is really sore today. I realized that he is definitely getting into "old age," as much as I didn't want to see it before. Amelia came over as soon as I told her and did a quick triage. Luckily, we are both off work for the holiday and I'm not on call, so I was here to help him open the restaurant and get all the food out to the customers. It was really busy because of the holiday, too.

Liberty Falls set off fireworks last night, and I wish you could have been here. Next year. You have got to be exhausted being gone this long. Again, my imagination fails me.

Love,
H.

January 22nd, 2123
Liberty Falls, VT

Andrew,

We're having a girl!

This is in the baby book along with all the other details, but I am so excited I wanted to repeat myself. The ultrasound Dr. Lowell did today was very clear.

I have spent a lot of time writing down lists of possible names in the baby book and trying to make up my mind, but in the end, I decided on Phoebe. Phoebe Grayson-Halley. She is healthy and moving a lot on the ultrasound. My baby bump has grown into a bulge. I hope the Reserves don't call me out to any formal events that require dress uniform, because mine won't fit anymore at this point.

Love,
H.

February 13th, 2123
Liberty Falls, VT

Andrew,

Happy 37th birthday! Wherever you are, I hope you are safe.

I'm still in the loop, of course, and Colonel Harris gives me occasional updates about the progress the Fleet is making. Also, *Wellington* <u>finally</u> managed to launch. What an unlucky ship. I doubt they'll find too many volunteers willing to serve on her. You know how superstitious many in the Fleet are.

This is in the baby book, but it's exciting, so I'm writing it again: I can feel Phoebe moving sometimes—just little flutters right now, but definitely noticeable. You have no idea how strange and yet comfortable that feels at the same time. Jennifer says the movements will get stronger pretty quickly. I have all the ultrasound recordings from the FB, but all my care is now with Dr. Lowell and she's adding to those recordings, so you'll get to see everything I'm seeing right now eventually.

I'm having some cake for you tonight. Pregnancy cravings are real—I never used to have much of a sweet tooth, but now I find myself cycling through the dessert menu at the Chief's every evening. I'm watching your suit telemetry again in the background. I know it by heart, but hearing your voice fools my brain into a kind of contentment. And hearing your exchange with Elin fills me with surety every time. You are coming home to me.

I love you.
H.

February 25th, 2123
Liberty Falls, VT

Andrew,

It's been two years to the day since *Jo'burg* saw *Washington* disappear from the plot. The Science people are positive that you went through that barely detectable wormhole the Lankies use to travel from and to Capella. None of the probes have come back through that wormhole yet, and nobody knows why.

Gods, I wish Evelyn was still alive. I wish you were here. But if wishing did anything, I wouldn't still be having this one-sided conversation with you.

I'm pretty large now, and I have a maternity wardrobe, starting with the tunic Amelia gave me. I can't fit in any of my uniforms right now, not even the loose cammies. The trauma center sprang for a bigger flight suit so I can keep doing my shifts, but at some point I'll have to take leave because I physically won't fit behind the controls anymore. I wish you were here to laugh at the mirror with me. The trauma center flight suit is orange, which is fitting because that's also my general shape now.

Love,
H.

March 11th, 2123
Joint Base Goose Bay

Andrew,

    I got orders Friday to report to Goose Bay for familiarization on new drop ships, so I've been there for a few days. ATS-13, my old outfit, is at Goose Bay at the moment as well, and Colonel Harris came to see me and check in, which is nice. I'm still not used to competent and caring COs.

    The new drop ships aren't ours. They're fresh designs the PacAlliance cooked up for their Avengers. I love the Dragonfly, but I have to admit to some serious tech envy. Their drop ships are called the Hayabusa class—it's the Japanese name for the peregrine falcon, the fastest bird in the world. The name fits the ships, let me tell you. They're sleek and mean-looking, and they have tech that's better than ours in some ways. The PacAlliance pilots showed off their new birds and did some ground attack runs at the live-fire range. I don't think the Fleet had any idea about my pregnancy yet because I got a lot of surprised looks when I showed up. Some of the NAC pilots got to tag along in the co-pilot seats for the gun runs, but they wouldn't let me fly even though I am still qualified and on active flight status with the trauma center. I was a little jealous, but in the end it's probably not a good idea to subject a fetus to possible high-g maneuvers or emergency ejection.

    Since I was ground-bound, I had time to let my old CO catch me up on the Fleet's recon efforts. We now have sensors full time and stealth ships occasionally on station in Capella, 51 Pegasi, and 26 Draconis. It doesn't take a great tactical genius to figure out that those last two are the systems they'll try to take back first once we go back on the offensive. Part of me still wants to be there when it happens, but that voice is getting quieter with every passing month, especially as Phoebe keeps getting larger, doing stuff to my body that isn't compatible with active duty.

Love,
H.

March 25th, 2123
Liberty Falls, VT

Andrew,

Something good and bad happened today. Fleet transferred your bonus and your retirement money to the accounts I had designated over a year ago. That will pay for the house completely. That's good, of course, but I have mixed feelings about it. There's a finality to that transaction because the Fleet officially wrote you off.

I halfway believed they wouldn't release the money because of your classified mission—that they knew *Washington* was still on a covert deployment, and they just couldn't tell anyone, not even the next of kin. I don't want to ponder what I should believe now, logically. I am choosing to continue to believe you are still coming back to me, even if Fleet doesn't. I know that's what you are trying to do.

I'll wait for you, no matter how long it takes, Andrew, and I'll have surprises for you when you get here, surprises that you are going to love.

Love,
H.

April 10th, 2123
Liberty Falls, VT

Andrew,

Now that it's spring, and mud season is drying up, they're about to resume construction on our house. It should be finished before Phoebe is born.

I cannot wait to see your face when you come home to Liberty Falls. It's a different world for you now.

I keep getting bigger and more uncomfortable by the day. One thing hardly anyone mentions when they talk about the miracle of pregnancy is how you have to run to the head much more frequently (or waddle, as the case may be.) Turns out that when you have a baby doing headstands on your bladder, incontinence becomes a regular thing. Glamorous, I know.

And that pregnancy glow people talk about? That's just sweat, most of the time.

Love,
H.

May 1st, 2123
Liberty Falls, VT

Andrew,

Chief Kopka turned sixty today. He wouldn't tell me when his birthday was last year and I had to trick him into it this year, but I was crafty and he slipped up. I actually made the cake when he was out on some errands yesterday and I had to hide it in his walk-in refrigerator. I invited our friends, including Amelia, to the restaurant after the dinner service. We had a little celebration despite his direct orders. I told him that I outrank him, and that my orders are for him to enjoy the day, the cake, and the company. When we told him to blow out the candle and make a wish, he just looked at me and gave me a knowing little wink.

I'm glad you found him so many years ago, Andrew, and that I ended up here thanks to that chance meeting. Without the people I have in my life now, I don't know what I would have done when everything was just darkness and despair. I still don't feel entirely whole, and that won't change until you're back with me. But at least I no longer feel broken.

Love,
H.

May 14th, 2123
Liberty Falls, VT

Andrew,

All the appliances were installed in our house today. It's coming together, and everything will be finished when Phoebe decides to come out. She's due on June 9th, but Jennifer says that can vary widely. Babies sometimes come early, sometimes late, seldom on time.

I wish you were here to share in these experiences! This journal and the baby book will have to be enough when you finally get to read them. You have got to be so ready to be home.

Love,
H.

May 22nd, 2123
Liberty Falls, VT

Andrew,

The contractors just wrapped up final trim work in the house today. All the trucks and tools are gone, the lights work, and the water is running. I am so pleased with how it turned out. But it's completely empty. All the furniture, dishes, and all the other basic things that houses need will get delivered over the next few days.

Tomorrow, I'm cleaning this house top to bottom. The contractors picked up after themselves, but they weren't as thorough as I would have liked. There's still dirt and sawdust in too many places. And the yard is barren, covered with straw. I am told the grass will pop up any time, and that I'll be sorry I wished for it because then it will need to be mowed. Of all the things I imagined I'd do in my life, mowing a lawn was not on that list.

Love,
H.

June 3rd, 2123
Liberty Falls, VT

Andrew,

I'm having false labor pains and contractions, called Braxton-Hicks contractions. Jennifer came as soon as I called her. The Chief was here when she arrived. She says it's just my body getting ready for delivery. She advised that I initiate my maternity leave ASAP because I could move to real delivery at any moment. I'll put in for it tomorrow.

Love,
H.

June 5th, 2123
Liberty Falls, VT

Andrew,

The final furniture delivery arrived today—just in time, I think. Phoebe's due in 4 days, but she'll come when she wants to come, Jennifer says, and I am so ready. I have never felt so heavy, so ponderous. It's like being on a world with twice Earth's gravity, while having your legs loosely tethered to each other and carrying a beachball filled with sand.

Luckily, I started maternity leave yesterday because of those false labor pains, so I won't have to drag myself into a medevac bird for a while.

My official leave goes until September, but Dr. Lowell has to sign off on my return, so the actual date I return to work is up to her.

I can't wait for you to be here!

Love,
H.

June 15th, 2123
Burlington, VT

Andrew,

I am in the hospital right now, in the maternity ward. Your daughter was born several hours ago. I will fill in all the details in the baby book, of course, but I couldn't skip this entry in this journal.

She arrived in the world 6 days later than she could have with a mohawk of dark hair, and she aced every sign of neonatal health on Dr. Lowell's tests. I am doing perfectly fine, and we'll be going home tomorrow to use the nursery for the first time. I am beyond ready for you to get home and experience all the joy that is waiting for you.

Andrew, I want another. If you were here, you would, too. When I actually laid eyes on her in real life for the first time, a feeling came over me that I have never experienced in my life. It was the most tender, loving, voracious, and utterly whole sensation, as contradictory as some of that sounds. I suspect you would have felt it, too, if you were here. But what it hit me with instantly and left me with was this: I want another. That's probably the hormones talking, but it's real.

Love,
H.

July 10th, 2123
Liberty Falls, VT

Andrew,

Phoebe is the most beautiful baby in the world. She is so cute, so funny, so everything. It's incredible.

I started yet another journal to keep track of her development. I am constantly busy right now, so very bound to all her needs. I'm only free at nap time, and I usually need a nap when she does. So I haven't written in this journal for a little while. I'm writing a lot in the newest book, so you're going to have a lot of reading to do when you get home.

I invited my father to come visit me in our home. He arrives by maglev in Burlington in a few hours. He doesn't know about Phoebe or the Chief, so he's going to be completely overcome. I'm okay with that because I will be, too, I suspect.

Love,
H.

July 13th, 2123
Liberty Falls, VT

Andrew,

Dad just left. He will visit again, and now he's actually talking about moving up here. He divorced my mother and moved out of their house into a condo. He has nothing else but work to look forward to at this point.

When he saw Phoebe for the first time, he seemed to go through the whole gamut of emotions I felt when she was born. Pure love. It was so moving to watch that it made me feel guilty.

I told him about the Chief and all he has done for us over the years, being my stand-in father. They met here the day before yesterday, and Dad genuinely thanked the Chief for his friendship and support of me. It went better than I had anticipated, and far better than I had feared. When Dad shook the Chief's hand, he actually cried, which made the Chief tear up, which made me cry too. Fucking hormones.

I'm not entirely sure what the outcome of all this will be in the end, but I think Dad will be in our lives in the future.

Love,
H.

August 10th, 2123
Liberty Falls, VT

Andrew,

Happy 11th Anniversary, my love. Your absence makes a bigger hole in my heart every year, but the pain is especially sharp on this day.

When you get back to me, I won't let the Fleet have you back. We've done our part. Now we should be able to live what's left of our lives in peace.

I love you,
H.

November 18th, 2123
Liberty Falls, VT

Andrew,

Today is my 37th birthday. I'm creeping ever closer to the dreaded four-oh.

I am not sure how much longer I'll be able to have children, but I assume it will be a few years yet before it gets too risky. There are two more fertilized eggs in the FB's cryovault. I think I want to bring them to full life before I am past the point where I can safely carry them to term. I would hate to miss out on another Phoebe in my life.

You and I are both only children, so I don't know how it is to have a sibling, but I think I could really have used one these last few years.

Love,
H.

February 13th, 2124
Liberty Falls, VT

Andrew,

Happy 38th birthday, my love.

Somewhere out there, you've just turned another year older without me. I don't want to miss any more of your birthdays, Andrew. I know you're not part of the ship's command staff, but also I know you're using every bit of pull you have to get home. I know you don't want to keep spending birthdays away from me. Those are the things I do know, and I am holding on to them because there's nothing else I can hold on to.

Wherever you are, I hope you feel my love for you.
H.

April 7th, 2124
Liberty Falls, VT

Andrew,

A *Washington* crash buoy just popped into the Solar system at the in-bound Capella node.

My PDP received that alert several hours ago, and I have been unable to do anything but read and reread it. There is no other news. My adrenaline is through the roof, and I'm shaking from it. I took the rest off the day off work. I'm not safe behind the stick right now.

I don't know if we have any ships on station in Capella, or <u>anything</u> else. I don't know how long it will take the Fleet to respond. I don't know why *Washington* sent a crash buoy. I don't know a goddamn thing other than the fact that your ship's crash buoy just came home.

I have never regretted leaving active duty until just now, only because I'd still be tied into MilNet. I sent a message to Colonel Harris and practically begged him for information, and I'm just waiting for a response.

Please be alive. That's all I'm asking of the universe right now.

Love,
H.

April 13th, 2124
Liberty Falls, VT

Andrew,

 You're back!

We ended our vidcall three hours ago, but I've only now pulled myself together enough to make this journal entry. It has been a long, long, long six days since *Washington* released its crash buoy. That wait was a more painful one than the past three years have been, knowing *Washington* was back but having no word from or about you. Colonel Harris only knew that *Wellington* had responded to the buoy. Otherwise, there was no message from Fleet for your wife, nothing popping up on my PDP for Reserve forces, no Fleet-wide information. Only silence. I couldn't send a message to you because your MilNet node was deleted last year.

But you're back!

I can't believe I finally get to type those words: you're back. You're back. You're back. I want to write it out a million times.

As soon as Fleet cut us off, I called the Chief and told him to come over instead of waking Phoebe and rushing to see him. The restaurant is closed today, so he was free. I met him outside, and he was instantly concerned because my face was all red and puffy. He thought I had gotten notice that you were dead after the news of the crash buoy.

When I told him that you're back in the Solar System and that I had spoken to you, we both sobbed like babies. We stayed outside so we wouldn't wake Phoebe. It's been a beautiful day, but now it's beyond gorgeous. Everything is more intense to me all of a sudden—sights, sounds, smells. It's like my all senses have been dialed up to their full settings for the first time in three years.

I have been unable to sit still for long since our talk, but the first thing I did was put in for time off from work, effective as soon as you arrive. Everyone knows you've been missing and no one knows why yet, so no one will doubt my need for family leave. I can't even begin to imagine what you've been through, but I'll be here every day to help you deal with it, for however long it takes.

<u>You're back.</u>

I've waited for this moment for so long, and now that it's finally here, it feels surreal, like I'm moving in one of those dreams where you know it's a dream but you can't quite shake yourself out of it. But if it really is a dream, I don't ever want to wake up.

I'll see you very soon.

Love,

H.

April 19th, 2124
Liberty Falls, VT

Andrew,

I am about to get Phoebe and myself dressed for our walk to the maglev station to meet you. Until now, there was a little voice in my head trying to seed doubt—that the unlucky *Wellington* would have a malfunction on the way, or that the Lankies would follow you into the system and shoot you out of space, or that the maglev train would crash even as you're on the way home. But I finally managed to shut that bitch up. Right now I am so giddy that I can barely type straight. I'll be seeing you in thirty minutes, and then my world will be whole again.

Thirty minutes. It seems silly to fret over them after all the time I've had to spend waiting, but I know they'll be the longest thirty minutes of my life.

Love,
H.

April 20th, 2124
Liberty Falls, VT

Andrew,

You are sound asleep in our bedroom as I write this. I had to get up to change Phoebe and put her back to sleep, and now I am wide awake, so I made some tea and sat down to write down my thoughts.

When I saw your face again at the station for the first time in three years, it felt like the world had suddenly righted itself, and the piece of my heart that has been missing for all this time slipped back into place.

When the Fleet shrink told me to start this journal, I had my doubts about the usefulness of the whole exercise. As I have written before, it seemed pointless and awkward at first. I'm glad I stuck with it, though, because this has helped so much to keep me sane over the years. It gave me a safe space to vent, and it was a way to connect to you even if all the entries only ever went one way.

When I read those older entries now, I'm grateful for the urge to write them down at the time because everything was such a mess for so long that it would all be lost in a general memory fog now if I hadn't typed it up. But now that you're back, I think this journal file has served its purpose. I'll probably start another one—it's too much of a habit now—but it will be for the events of our new life, not the sorrows of my old one. And a new life it is.

Signing off,
H.

June 15th, 2124
Liberty Falls, VT

Dear Phoebe,

Happy birthday, my beautiful girl! You are one year old today.

Your Papa is back in our lives, and I'm so glad you'll never remember a time when he wasn't there with us. He is no longer on combat duty, and you will never have to see him off on a deployment. I am beyond happy for all three of us, but especially for you because you will never have to experience that kind of all-consuming worry I lived with for over three years.

I closed this journal last month the day after your Papa came home to us, but today I decided to add a final entry. This journal was for me, but I know that one day you'll be old enough to want to know what happened, and then this file will be yours. I hope it will give you insight into your parents—who they were and why they did what they did—and maybe help you understand yourself better as well.

I am closing this file again, this time for good. I don't know what will happen between now and the day when you read this. I hope it's only joy and laughter, and many stories of all our lives well-lived. But whatever happens in the future, know that you were loved from the beginning, by parents who loved each other deeply.

I plan to start taking you up the mountain soon, to the stargazing spot that's always been our favorite since long before you were born. I hope it'll still be there when you read this, and that you know it well by then. Next time you go up there and look at the stars, remember that your parents were once up among them—sometimes together, often apart, but always connected. I want you to know that as vast as the galaxy seems, there's no distance that we wouldn't cross for each other, and for you. And when we are gone, a part of us will still be out there, traveling the solar winds together. Come up to our spot and talk to us any time you want. We'll be there, and we'll listen.

With all my love,
Mama

<End of File>